I0651061

Hawley Smart

A False Start

A Novel: Vol. II.

Hawley Smart

A False Start
A Novel: Vol. II.

ISBN/EAN: 9783337031534

Printed in Europe, USA, Canada, Australia, Japan

Cover: Foto ©Andreas Hilbeck / pixelio.de

More available books at **www.hansebooks.com**

A FALSE START.

A Novel.

BY

HAWLEY SMART,

AUTHOR OF "BREEZIE LANGTON," "FROM POST TO FINISH,"
"THE GREAT TONTINE," ETC., ETC.

IN THREE VOLUMES.

VOL. II.

LONDON: CHAPMAN AND HALL
LIMITED
1887.

CONTENTS OF VOL. II.

CHAPTER XI.

CHAPTER XII.

CHAPTER XIII.

CHAPTER XIV.

ERRATA.—VOL. II.

Page 17, line 15, *for* "sherry and bitters or brandy-sodas" *read* "sherries and bitters or brandies and sodas."

Page 251, line 10, *for* "loss of husband" *read* "loss of her husband."

A FALSE START.

CHAPTER I.

THE CHESTERFIELDS.

BUT Maurice, though he might admit to his wife that he was in some way morally guilty of the charge preferred against him, was very indignant that Mesdames Maddox and Praun should have had the presumption to come down and lecture Bessie on the subject. He had quite made up his mind to submit to no comment on his conduct from anybody in Tunnleton but the Reverend Jacob Jarrow. If the rumour, as it infallibly

would, reached the ears of the rector, and
that gentleman deemed fit to speak to him
on the subject, well, he would acknowledge
that he had transgressed in some shape
though able to give an emphatic denial
to the direct charge. As for Bessie being
preached to on the subject that he would
allow from nobody breathing.

He avoided the club all the next day, and
contented himself with such news as he could
extract from the paper he took in. That
morning brought a visit from Mr. Rumford,
who, though quite respectful, was very
earnest in his request for something on account, and retired evidently but half-satisfied
with the promise that his account should be
settled in the course of the month.

The next day was Thursday, and, as
Maurice knew well, the Chesterfield Stakes
at Newmarket were decided that afternoon.
He determined not to go to the club, he

would wait patiently and learn his fate from his own paper the next morning. That afternoon he recognised what the excitement of wagering on races was, and how it was growing upon him, as dram-drinking or opium-eating might do, although he was innocent of actual betting. He went about his daily work as usual and did it, but in preoccupied fashion, for his mind was all the time dwelling on that sunshiny meeting at the back of the " Ditch," and wondering what had been the result of the struggle for the " Chesterfields."

"It's terrible!" he muttered at last. "Do what I will I cannot throw this thing upon one side; we may restrain our passions, but we cannot control our thoughts. 1 wish Bessie's uncle had given her some other wedding present. I do believe—I do believe it will end in making the Church an impossible profession for me. I am getting

so infatuated with it, that I could quite
fancy my being so carried away as to resign
my curacy, and actually take to attending
race meetings. I know—no one better—
that it means nothing but ruin to a poor
man! that scores every year perish under
the wheels of the Turf Juggurnauth. Absurd!
I *must* shake it off."

He struck across the common, turned
down one of the innumerable country lanes
all fragrant with the scent of the hay and
the summer flowers, and stretched manfully
away for a couple of miles or so; but it was
of no use. All the way a fiend seemed
whispering in his ear " What has won the
' Chesterfields ? ' " He turned his face
homewards, and still, as if keeping time
with his footsteps, came the whispered—
" What—has—won—the—' Chesterfields ' ?"
All across the common it was the same thing.
He had determined not to go into the club,

but at last he told himself that it would be better *to know*, than to have this irritating question ringing continuously in his ears. He broke his resolution turned into the club, and was a little disconcerted at finding the sporting *coterie* gathered together in the hall. He passed rapidly through them without glancing at the telegram board, and made his way to the morning-room. There he sat down, and affected to read the papers. He had made up his mind what to do now. He would wait there for a bit. It was getting on towards six; a little later and the group in the hall would have doubtless dispersed, and he would then be able to look at the telegram board unnoticed.

For half-an-hour he fidgeted with the papers, and then taking his hat he left the room. As he had expected, the hall was now clear. No one was there to see him walk

quickly up to the board. His heart gave a
great jump as he gazed at the tissue.

Wandering Nun . . 1

Bajazet 2

Rocket 3

Won in a canter.

He rushed out of the club and hurried
towards home. What did this mean to him?
He hardly dared to think. John Madingley
had distinctly said that Bessie was to go
halves in all that accrued from the Wandering Nun's racing career. He knew that the
" Chesterfields " was a good stake—did that
mean that Bessie was entitled to half of it?
If so this probably meant some three or four
hundreds. What a windfall it would be for
them in their present circumstances; it
would obviate the touching of that money
which he had settled on Bessie; he would be
able to pay off his tradespeople, and to give
Badger something considerable on account.

"How late you are, Maurice!" exclaimed Bessie as he entered the drawing-room; "what can have kept you?"

"Well," he replied, "I felt I wanted a good long walk, so I went for a stretch out Blythfield way, and as I came back just looked in at the club; that remarkable filly of your uncle's, in which you are supposed to have a vested interest, has won a big race at Newmarket; whether that means anything to you or not, of course I do not know."

"I am sure I don't," replied Bessie; "but I should think probably it means a present of some sort; Uncle John is a man who doesn't talk at random, but always means what he says. But I wish, Maurice, you were not so interested in racing."

"I'm going to drop it from this out,' replied Maurice, "but I could not help a feverish anxiety to see if " The Wandering

Nun " won to-day at Newmarket. Well,
she has, and now I will shut my eyes to
her further proceedings."

As might have been expected, the mal-
practices of his curate were speedily reported to Mr. Jarrow. To do that gentleman
justice he manifested considerable incredulity.

" It may be as you say, General Maddox,
and I shall regret very much if it is so,
but I can hardly believe that a man of
refined, cultivated taste, like Mr. Enderby,
should fritter away his talents on such a
profitless and unintellectual pursuit as
horse-racing. Mr. Enderby entered at once
into all the incisive logic and satire of
the Verity Letters, and has besides literary
ambitions of his own. Some of his work
which I have had the privilege of perusing
is, I assure you, very passable indeed for a
young hand. He is most attentive to his

parish duties, and, though he is certainly
not so popular in the pulpit as Mr. Lomax,
yet I think there is more stuff in his sermons.
Of course I shall speak to him on the subject; it is only right that a man should
have a chance of refuting a scandal such
as this is, for a scandal it is to one of our
cloth. He may not know that the report
is afloat concerning him."

"I feel sure he is perfectly aware of it,"
replied the general sententiously, "and he
has taken no steps to justify himself in
any way."

The Reverend Mr. Jarrow was a pompous
and not particularly wise man, but one
thing he was always quite clear about, namely,
that the Church was not to be hectored over or
dictated to by the laity. He was as arbitrary
and jealous of the powers of the Church as
Cardinal Wolsey, and tolerated no interference
with his parish on the part of any of his

parishioners. He was well to do, having a
comfortable private income besides his living,
and was no niggard with regard to the
spending of money on his cure, but he
invited no co-operation on the part of the
wealthier of his flock that was not to be
under his immediate control. He had spent
and raised money to decorate his church
and improve his schools, but he had sted-
fastly insisted upon dictating as to how it
should be expended. He was sure to stand
by any curate of his who was attacked by
the laity, more especially when the charge
was proffered by one of the chiefs of that
military hierarchy at whose presence in
Tunnleton the reverend gentleman so persistently chafed.

It was the week succeeding the Newmarket races that General Maddox spoke
to Mr. Jarrow. The general was of course
aware of what had taken place between his

wife and Mrs. Enderby, and was quite as indignant on his part as Maurice was. He considered it a great piece of condescension that Mrs. Maddox should have taken the trouble to call upon Mrs. Enderby, acquaint her with her husband's iniquities, and implore her to use her influence to turn him from the error of his ways.

"I should like to know what more a kind-hearted woman could have done, and, by Jove, instead of being grateful, Mrs. Enderby actually flouts her, flouts her, sir, flouts my wife, Mrs. Maddox."

In fact, the two generals were both furious, and went about trumpeting in their wrath like wild elephants. A version of the scene in Mrs. Enderby's drawing room was all over the town by this time, and it was generally known that lady had behaved with extreme rudeness to Mrs. Maddox and Mrs. Praun simply because they had endeavoured

to persuade her to exercise her influence over
her husband to induce him to refrain from
speculation on horse-racing. The tide was
running strong against the Enderbys. The
Torkeslys and other members of the community expressed their opinion that there
was nothing for Mr. Enderby but to resign,
he could never hope to be of any use in his
vocation at Tunnleton. Dick Madingley
took advantage of the popular outcry against
the curate to throw his stone at him. He
had made up his difference with Kinnersley,
and finding that he was a stanch believer in
Madingley was careful what he said before
him. But Kinnersley, not being present, he
did not scruple to remark to that sporting
coterie of which he was the acknowledged
oracle,

    " He's a knowing shot the parson. I don't
know where he got his inspiration, but Mr.
Brooks's Wandering Nun for the 'Chester-

fields' was about one of the best things of the season. He don't bet, not he, oh no. Quite right to say so in his position, and I was a fool to chaff him about it. All the fault of that confounded sherry and bitters. Dashed if I don't think they distil that sherry on the premises, it is so strong. But you can't make me believe he hadn't a pretty good win over it, I've seen rather to much of life for that. It's not in human nature to have such a bit of information and not make money of it."

Mr. Madingley, I am afraid, had considerable experience of the shady side of life, and was far from placing a high estimate on the morality of his fellows.

But the Enderbys were by no means friendless, and the Chyltons, with whom they had been intimate from the first, stood gallantly by them now. Frank Chylton, when the rumour first reached his cars, said stoutly, he did not believe it, and then went straight to Maurice and told him what people were saying concerning him.

"There is not a word of truth in it," rejoined the curate. "I may have given some little handle for such a falsehood to get about by foolishly talking about racing to some of the men at the club, but I have never made a bet of any description since I left the University, which was before I was married."

"It is very odd such a report should have got about," replied Frank, "but I felt sure it was false before I saw you, and now I have your own word for it I shall give it the most unqualified contradiction wherever I hear it alluded to."

The Reverend Mr. Jarrow took an early opportunity of speaking to his curate about this unfortunate rumour as he termed it, and Maurice answered him as frankly as he had done Chylton.

"Ah, Mr. Enderby, I felt sure I could

rely upon you, and I shall have the greatest possible pleasure in requesting General Maddox not to intrude upon my valuable time with such idle *canards* in future. A venial imprudence you may have been guilty of, but that is a very different thing from the accusation they would fain lay at your door. I would recommend you to be a little more guarded all the same in future," and the rector departed, burning to tackle General Maddox and demand retractation of his charges on that gentleman's part.

A veritable storm in a tea-cup all this, no doubt, but it is precisely such little convulsions that constitute the salt of existence in small country towns. Questions of the kind are to them what a strenuous battle between the Government and the Opposition may be in the House of Commons, and Tunnleton was literally divided into two camps on the subject of Maurice Enderby's iniquities. Generals Maddox and Praun were the leaders of one party, who received the assertion of his innocence with polite incredulity, while the Reverend Mr. Jarrow and Frank Chylton championed him with perhaps more zeal than discretion. Singularly enough, too, there was quite a bitter feeling engendered on the subject amongst the community, for, while the one side held that if you believed in Mr. Enderby's innocence, well, then, you would probably believe anything, the other contended that you must be malicious, spiteful, and uncharitable if you doubted the word of a gentleman of unblemished repute.

Nobody, perhaps, contributed more to keep the scandal alive than Mr. Richard Madingley. He was a very popular character in Tunnleton just now, as a well-to-do young bachelor who entertained liberally might well be. There were very few young

ladies in the town who would not have
thought twice before saying no to an offer
of occupying the top of his table for life.
Dick Madingley was quite aware of this,
and gave himself great airs in society in
consequence, and society bore with them, as
it usually does with the impertinences
of young gentlemen of substance.

We have so far seen Madingley under
rather unfavourable circumstances, but it
must not be supposed that his manner was
so coarse and obtrusive generally as it had
been in the Tunnleton Club. *In vino veritas*
is a very true saying, and it is probable that
sherry-and-bitters or brandy-sodas had much
to say to his want of breeding upon those
occasions; still, upon this topic of Enderby's
offending he had always something to say;
he was as vindictive a man as ever stepped,
and had never forgiven Enderby's rebuff in
the billiard-room.

" My dear Miss Torkesly," he would say, " don't ask me what I think; as a man of the world, when a gentleman informs me that a horse, that has never run, will win a big race, I invariably conclude he is in possession of private information; when I see him feverishly anxious about the betting previous to that race, and about the result, I can only conclude that he has very naturally made use of his information. Whether that is a right thing to do for a clergyman I don't pretend to determine; it's a question I leave to older heads than mine."

This was the line that Mr. Madingley adopted,

" The evidence is all against him but still I will not say he is guilty."

It was two days after Maurice's interview with Mr. Jarrow that, upon coming down to breakfast, he found Bessie seated at the table, an open letter in her hand, and a face in which surprise, exultation, and dismay were strangely mingled.

"Maurice," she said, "I have got a letter from Uncle John, and I don't quite know whether to be pleased or sorry about it."

"From Uncle John? Let me see it."

She handed him the letter without another word.

"MY DEAR BESSIE,

"Our joint property has turned out a veritable flyer, and I honestly believe just now is about the best two-year-old in England. The Wandering Nun won her race last week at Newmarket with consummate ease, and there were some very fair youngsters behind her.

"I hope you and your husband like Tunnleton, and are pretty comfortable there. It is many years ago since I saw it—more years indeed than I care to think

c 2

of. I recollect it is very pretty but very quiet.

" I inclose you a cheque for your half of the Chesterfields, and trust that if she goes on well the Nun will prove a gold-mine to both of us.

" Best love to yourself, and with kind regards to your husband,

" Believe me,

" Ever, dear Bessie,

" Your affectionate Uncle,

" JOHN MADINGLEY."

" And what's the cheque for ? " asked Maurice.

" Here it is," she replied, handing it him.

Maurice quite started as he gazed upon it. " Five hundred and fifty-seven pounds," he murmured slowly.

CHAPTER II.

EDITH MOLECOMBE.

"What did you mean by saying you didn't know whether to be glad or sorry?" asked Maurice, as soon as he had recovered from his first surprise.

"It looks rather as if the charge brought against you by these two terrible women was true, doesn't it?"

"It does rather," replied Maurice, smiling, as he dropped the cheque into his waistcoat-pocket, "but we know that it is not so.

I have a perfectly clear conscience on that
score, and just think, Bessie, what we can do
with the money.   It will put us perfectly
straight with the Tunnleton tradespeople—no
bother about writing to your trustees now,
my dear—enable me to stop Badger's mouth
with a handsome cheque on account, and
leave us a comfortable balance besides in the
local bank.

"But what will Mr. Chylton think when
you cash the cheque, Maurice ?   You know
you have never told him anything about
Uncle John's wedding present.   He believes
thoroughly in you, but the presenting such a
big cheque as this on the top of this charge
will look so dreadfully as if you had won the
money by betting."

"What a clever little woman it is !" rejoined Maurice, admiringly.   "You are
right; it would.   I will take it up and get
it cashed at my banker's in town."

This Maurice accordingly did, but he then committed the strange oversight of paying two hundred pounds into his account at the Tunnleton Bank. This was even more likely to induce the people at the bank to put a false construction on his sudden acquirement of money than if he had put in John Madingley's cheque. The story of the sporting parson who had won such a good stake over the Chesterfields was by this well known to the inferior strata of Tunnleton; the bank clerks looked upon Maurice, not with the horror of Generals Maddox and Praun, but with no little admiration. The ostlers and the fly-drivers had by this time heard of Mr. Enderby as a rare judge of racing, and accorded him no little veneration in consequence. He had mounted a far higher pinnacle in the eyes of these godless understrappers of the stable than any eloquence in the pulpit could ever have placed

him on. Sad to say, they took more interest
in the ways of this world than in the pre-
paring of themselves for another.

Mr. Rumford, the butcher, and his brethren,
when they found all their arrears promptly
discharged, were similarly convinced that the
report of Mr. Enderby's racing proclivities
was true, and these good people received it
and looked upon it in very different lights;
some of them laughed, and thought a sporting curate rather a joke than otherwise; but
there were other more straitlaced who shook
their heads at the idea of a clergyman
dabbling in such a pursuit; the opinion
of these latter somewhat mollified by the
comforting fact that they had at all events
got their money. In short, at the end of a
fortnight from that Newmarket week Maurice Enderby might as well have endeavoured to convert the betting-ring as to
induce the bulk of Tunnleton to believe that

he did not bet upon races. Even his stanch friend Frank Chylton was staggered; he naturally knew that Maurice had paid in two hundred pounds to his account, and in face of the charge brought against him there could be no doubt that this was a most suspicious circumstance; he was loyal to his friend as ever, but did think that out of consideration for those who were standing by him Maurice should be more prudent. Frank saw at once that the payment of this two hundred would be known to all the clerks in the bank, and, though his subordinates knew very well that keeping their mouths closed was rigorously exacted by their position, he had no doubt that with such a titillating piece of scandal flying about the town they would never be able to refrain from contributing their quota to it.

Maurice, in the mean time, pursued the even tenour of his way. He had laid out

his windfall exactly as he had contemplated.
Mr. Badger was profuse in his acknowledg-
ments, and his tradesmen were all *chapeau
bas*, and that balance at the bank was a comforting thing to think upon ; but for all that
he could not disguise from himself that a
considerable portion of Tunuleton society
gave him the cold shoulder. Their greetings
were chilly, and he was apt to find himself
left out of the delirious gaieties of that centre
of the universe. One of his enemies there
was who certainly retired from the fray
sore discomfited. In an ill-advised moment
General Maddóx took upon himself to read
this contumacious young man a lesson on
manners.

I don't think the general ever forgot that
fall, and, were he alive, I think, would even
still give a slight shudder at hearing Maurice
Enderby's name mentioned. It took place
in the club, though not before witnesses.

General Maddox was far too gentlemanly a man to have spoken as he did except in private.

" Mr. Enderby ! er, er ! you'll excuse my mentioning it, but when a lady of Mrs. Maddox's position takes the trouble to call upon Mrs. Enderby, with the kind view of tendering her some good advice, I really think she is entitled to be treated with civility and consideration."

Maurice's face hardened, and there was a dangerous glitter in his eye as he replied,

" Mrs. Maddox, sir, entered Mrs. Enderby's drawing-room apparently to malign her husband; she was ruder, as was also Mrs. Praun, than I had believed it possible that any lady could be. I have further to point out that my private affairs are no business of yours, and I will trouble you not to meddle with them for the future."

"Sir!" exclaimed General Maddox, "do you mean to insinuate ——."

"I insinuate nothing," interposed Maurice quickly. "I have said what I meant to say, and am now going to lunch, and have the honour to wish you good morning."

As for General Maddox, he sank back in an arm-chair, gasping with indignation. His usual portly presence was in a state of collapse pitiable to witness; it was probably a quarter of a century since any one had presumed to tackle the pompous old general in this fashion.

"By Jupiter! I'll have him out," he muttered at last, ignoring for the moment that the duel was as obsolete in England as the tilt-yard, and that even in its most flourishing days the priest's cassock carried exemption. After a little he got up, and as he walked home said, "No! there is only one

thing to do, hunt the fellow out of Tunnleton; and, by Jupiter! I'll do it."

The glorious July days rolled sunnily by,
and the country around Tunnleton is in all
its glory. The woods and fields are full of
wild flowers, and the hedges thick with dog-
roses and wild honey-suckle, the meadows
alive with sturdy lambs, and the corn, though
standing strong and green upon the ground,
yet here and there begins to show slight
indications of changing to a golden hue.

The parade is deserted, and nothing but
the severe exigencies of shopping bring the
fair ladies of Tunnleton to the High Street.
The hum of insects is in the air, the very
birds give vent to low querulous twitterings
as if entering their protest about the state of
the thermometer. The cattle stand languidly
switching their tails till the agressive army
of flies proves too much for their patience,
when they stampede in wild ungainly gallops

round their pastures. Tumbleton lies at the bottom of a basin, and consequently the little air there is barely reaches it. The shopkeepers stand sweltering in their shirt-sleeves at their doors; no one would think of buying and selling, save from dire necessity, in such weather. The dogs lie upon the door-steps with their lolling tongues and panting sides, mutely appealing in their canine breasts against the irony of dedicating such days peculiarly to them. It is one of those glorious old English summers such as are all but dim memories.

Tumbleton society has betaken itself to the open air. It is cricketing, lawn-tennising, picnicking, munching fruit and consuming claret-cup. There were perpetual open-air gatherings of one sort or another, and Maurice Enderby could not but see that from a great many of these his wife and himself were excluded; there could be no

doubt of it; people who had called upon them
in the first instance, and who had appeared
anxious to make their acquaintance, now
neglected to ask them to such entertainments as they might be giving. It did not
require much penetration to see that there
was a hostile influence at work, and that
he had made implacable enemies of the two
generals he felt no doubt. Of course, the
rector, his friends the Chyltons, and some
others welcomed him as cordially as of yore,
but amongst the people who had not exactly
dropped his acquaintance, but had apparently struck him off their invitation list,
Maurice was a little surprised to find the
Molecombes. Mr. Molecombe was the
senior partner in Molecombe and Chylton's
bank, and had, on Frank Chylton's repre-
sentation, been one of the first people to
call and offer civility to the Enderbys;
however, of the cause of their defection he
was destined to be speedily enlightened.

He was passing through the deserted
High Street on one of those errands that
formed part of his daily work, when he
encountered one of the Miss Torkeslys;
as before said, no one ever went out in
Tumnleton without meeting a Torkesly.

"Good morning, Mr. Enderby," she exclaimed, with all the volubility character-
istic of her race. "Have you heard the
news?"

"No," replied Maurice, as he shook hands;
"I was not aware that there was anything
stirring — not even a breeze," he added,
smiling.

"Oh yes, I assure you, Mr. Enderby, a
marriage—a real marriage. And I suppose
it will take place in the autumn. She is
such a nice girl and I am so fond of her.
I am going up now to congratulate her.
I am sure they must be pleased! A young
good-looking husband with lots of money,

what more could anyone want. I don't believe she cares much about him, you know. And I should think she is a good deal older than he is, but it will do all very well no doubt, and I am sure I am delighted. And, you know, it really was getting time dear Edith was settled."

"Excuse me, Miss Torkesly, but I really have no idea of whom you are speaking."

"No, I forgot you don't go about quite so much as you — I mean — that is, you gentlemen don't interest yourselves so much in marriages and engagements as we do."

"But won't you enlighten my ignorance?" replied Maurice.

"Of course, of course—you will be delighted to hear it, such friends as they are of yours, and you so intimate with the Chyltons, and all!"

Maurice said nothing. He felt that this feminine wind-bag must have its way.

"Yes," continued the young lady, complacently; "Edith Molecombe has accepted Mr. Madingley, and, of course, the wedding will be a very grand affair when it does come off; and I do hope they will ask us to the breakfast. Good morning. I really have no time to stand gossiping," and with a gracious smile and bend of her head Miss Torkesly resumed her weary pilgrimage— for the Molecombes lived about a mile outside the town, and under that fierce midday sun the walk thither was really no small sacrifice at the altar of friendship.

"Yes," muttered Maurice, as he strolled on, "that would easily account for the Molecombes dropping me. I know Mr. Madingley has never forgiven me for putting him down, and, without knowing anything positive about it, I should guess he had the capacity of being what Dr. Johnson admired, '*a good hater*,'" and then Maurice

thought later in the afternoon he would
stroll up to the Chyltons and have a talk
with them. So when the sun waxed low
in the heavens, dropping like a ball of fire
into his bed in the west, Maurice and his
wife started for the Chyltons. They lived
in a pretty villa standing in the middle of
a large garden. To say grounds would be
a misnomer, it was really nothing more
than an extensive garden—well shrubbed,
well treed, and tastefully laid out. Sitting
under a horse-chesnut on the verge of the
flower-gemmed lawn was Mrs. Chylton, a
tea-equipage at her side, and her two chil-
dren playing at her feet.

" I am so glad to see you, Bessie," she
cried, as she rose to welcome the new
comer, " and you too, Mr. Enderby. How
good of you to come up and lighten my
solitude! I was suffering from a bad headache in the early part of the afternoon, and

so give up all thoughts of the Molecombes'
garden-party. By the way, how is it that
you are not there ? "

" For the best of all possible reasons—we
were not asked," rejoined Bessie.

Mrs. Chylton said nothing more, but she
was a firm friend of the Enderbys, and
resolved to take the earliest opportunity of
favouring the Molecombe family with her
opinion on the subject.

" I suppose you were very much astonished at the announcement of Edith's
engagement ? " said she.

" Well, yes ; but, as I only know Mr.
Madingley by sight, I was not likely to
have any suspicion of what was coming."

" No," interposed Maurice, " and then, as
you know, Mrs. Chylton, in consequence of
my quarrel with Generals Maddox and
Praun, a good many houses in the place
are now closed to me."

"Yes, they no doubt have considerable influence in Tunnleton, and a certain number of people would be sure to take their side, but after the shameful conduct of their wives I don't see, Mr. Enderby, that you could have done anything else."

"No, a man cannot allow his wife to be insulted. General Maddox further had the presumption to attempt to lecture me upon keeping my wife in order."

"What!" cried Laura Chylton.

"He had. That really was the gist of a conversation he thought proper to commence with me when we found ourselves left together the next day in the morning-room of the club, but I don't think he is likely to try his hand at that again," and then Maurice gave Mrs. Chylton an account of that interview.

Mrs. Chylton burst out laughing when Maurice described with a good deal of

humour the conclusion of his passage of
arms with the general.

"Oh, Mr. Enderby!" she cried; "did
you really say that to him? He will never
forgive you. I don't suppose his dignity
has received such a shock for years; and
General Maddox without his dignity is
nothing. Frank must hear this—it will be
nearly the death of him; he'll be home from
the Molecombes about seven. If you can
put up with cold lamb and salad for dinner,
be good people and stop. It's not sermon
night, Mr. Enderby, so you have no
excuse."

"I shall be very glad indeed," said
Maurice.

"Now that's neighbourly," replied Laura.
"Smoke if you want to; you'll find the
papers and magazines in Frank's room.
Bessie and I are going to have a good long
lazy gossip."

CHAPTER III.

"WHAT A BORE I'VE BEEN."

FRANK CHYLTON came home to dinner, and, as his wife prophecied, laughed till the tears ran down his cheeks at Maurice's account of his skirmish with General Maddox.

"I don't blame you," he said; "old Maddox richly deserved it, but it isn't calculated to quench the ill-will with which he regards you. No, depend upon it, he and his immediate friends will make the very most of this trumped-up story, and they can,

to some extent, make the place unpleasant to
you, no doubt."

"We must endeavour to bear his enmity
with what resignation we can. If his friendship is to be burdened with a right to
administer advice on the part of Mrs. Maddox, I infinitely prefer to be without it—eh,
Bessie?"

"Yes," replied Mrs. Enderby, laughing
merrily, "I am quite content to figure as
the bad child who wouldn't take its powder
in spite of all assurances that it was for its
good. I suppose they were very full of
Edith's engagement this afternoon?"

"Yes, it was a perfect *feu de joie* of congratulations. She looked happy and conscious, and Madingley more at his ease and
less of a fool than a man usually does under
the circumstances."

"Is Mr. Molecombe very pleased, Frank?"
inquired his wife.

" Very, I should say—' Very satisfactory, good county family, heir to a nice property —yes, thank you, it will do, Chylton,' he replied, when I congratulated him. You know his short jerky manner of talking."

" Well, I suppose it is a good thing for her," rejoined Laura, " though personally I can't say I ever quite fancied Mr. Madingley—I can't tell you why, but it is so."

" I think I can, Mrs. Chylton, but pray put no particular stress upon my opinion, as I'll admit to being somewhat prejudiced against him. What you are conscious of is this—that Mr. Madingley is not quite a gentleman."

" You are right, Maurice," replied her husband. " He opened a very liberal account with us when he first came, and, as far as money is concerned, there is no reason to suppose but what he has plenty; but you're

right, it crops out whenever you have much
to do with him. Once get through the
French polish, and you'll find an arrogant
cad at the bottom of it."

"Come, Bessie," cried Laura Chylton,
laughing ; " when the gentlemen get so very
pronounced in their opinions, it is best to
leave them to themselves 'ere worse comes
of it."

"Now Maurice," said Frank, as soon as
the ladies had left the room, " I've something
on my mind concerning you. I hate mys-
teries and therefore I'm going to out with it
at once. I don't want in the least to pry
into your private affairs, but what induced
you in the face of this scandal to pay 200*l.*
into our bank last week? Of course, Molecombe knows it, and, forgive me if it sounds
like an impertinence, it is a big sum for a
man in your position to lodge to his account,
and I need hardly say gives additional

handle to the story of your having won money by horse-racing."

" Stupid of me ! " exclaimed Maurice, " I wanted cash to draw against, to satisfy my tradespeople; I came unexpectedly into some money, and, never thinking of the construction you have put upon it, paid into your bank."

Frank Chylton said nothing, but he looked uneasily at his companion. Maurice caught the glance, hesitated for a minute or two, and then said,

" You've been a stanch friend, Frank, and are entitled to know the whole story, and, providing you will give me your promise not to open your lips without my permission, I will tell it you."

Chylton readily gave the required promise, and then, without further preamble, Maurice related the story of Uncle John's eccentric wedding present, and what had come of it so far.

Frank listened attentively.

"I don't know anything about such things," he said, when Maurice had finished, "but how it led you to take an interest in racing matters is very easy of comprehension. In that respect it has been perhaps an unfortunate gift, but, so far as I do understand things, from a money point of view, it is likely to be very profitable. This successful filly has only just started on her career, and will probably win several more valuable races before she has done. I have only one thing to say, don't think that I'm preaching, but for heaven's sake don't place reliance on big cheques like this tumbling in. That would sap the marrow of any man's character, and it is after all the hazard of two or three years. It's moral gambling, Maurice, and your uncle had better have written you a cheque for five hundred right off than made Mrs. Enderby such an ill-omened present. Forgive me, old man. What a bore I have been ! Come and have a cigar on the lawn before you trot home."

It was a very pleasant hour that, in the garden, in the bright light of the full moon. Frank and Maurice strolled up and down enjoying their tobacco, and talking over their old boyish days, when Maurice used to come down to spend his Easter holidays at Tunnleton; while the ladies interchanged those confidences which it is seldom the sex has not at command. Ah, those boyish days ! I am not quite sure whether we ever experience the same pure, unadulterated enjoyment afterwards. I am not talking of school-days, in which there was more to loathe than to like, but of those holiday times when we were permitted our own sweet will, and were up at daybreak to take up the night-lines. Then

there were birds' nests and wasps' nests to be
taken in the morning, countless occupations
for the afternoon if our restless energies
were not expended, and rabbits to be potted
with the old single barrel we were allowed
in the gloaming. That grim piece of irony,
the holiday-task, did not exist in those days,
or if it did was a little joke between master
and boy, supposed to pacify parents in wet
weather, when their progeny made themselves more objectionable than usual in consequence of enforced confinement, but never
to be seriously alluded to on returning to
school.

As they walked home Maurice said to his
wife,

" I have had it clean out with Frank
Chylton, Bessie, and told him the whole
story. He a little staggered me ; he seems to
regard your uncle's as the gift of the wicked

fairy, and is a little disposed to take your view of it."

" Oh, I hope not, Maurice. I own I was afraid at first it was leading you to take an interest in matters that would be destructive, to say nothing of disgraceful, to your professional career. But you have given that up, have you not ? "

" Yes, but I'll admit the poison is hardly out of my blood. It is with great difficulty I abstain from the sporting papers, and in our own daily I never can resist the sporting intelligence. Is there inflammatory action in money that comes to one in this wise ? On my word, I am half-tempted to believe it. Bessie, Bessie, I am afraid this fatal present of Uncle John's will be the ruin of me ! "

" Nonsense, Maurice, dear, you're excited to-night and taking too strained a view of things. I know I took the theoretical and

high-toned view at first, but, oh, Maurice,
when it comes to the practice, there is no
denying there's a comfort in money that's
not dishonestly come by. To walk into
Rumford's shop now is so different to what
it was a fortnight ago. Take Uncle John's
present, as we should take it, as windfalls
by no manner of means to be reckoned on.
Don't trouble your head about the Wandering
Nun, and then, dear Maurice, no harm can
come to you."

Poor Bessie! She spoke as a woman will
speak, or, for the matter of that, men too,
about a thing outside her experience; as if
nine men out of ten, who have made a
tolerable bet on the Derby or drawn a
prominent favourite in a Derby sweep, do
not, more or less, speculate upon what they
will do with those imaginary winnings.
They may deny it, but I know better, and
have even had many invitations to dinners

from sanguine backers, dinners which, sad
to say for their sakes, were never celebrated.
When the Enderbys reached home they
found a heap of letters on their table; of
these, three only have anything to do with
this story, but with these three it is necessary the reader should be acquainted; one
was to Maurice, the others to his wife; we
will take Mrs. Enderby's first.

" My dear Bessie,

"You and I are halves in the greatest
flyer of the year. There will be another
sugar-plum fall into our mouths, I think, at
Goodwood, and perhaps something more
later on, though you know racing is both,
like life, uncertain and desperately wicked.
You must forgive an old man, my dear;
people were laxer in their ideas when I was
young, and I am too old to change; I've
done and do my duty conscientiously in my

own way, but my ways, I know, are not in accordance with the times.

" What I am writing to you chiefly about is this. Can you put up with an old, somewhat irritable, old man after Goodwood ? I am ordered change and quiet, and, though I have no business to be seen on a race-course, must go there to see my favourite run. Tunnleton suited me years ago, and the doctors tell me will now, and that the iron-water is just the tonic I require. They must say something, but of course what I do require is the hands of the clock put back a quarter of a century.

" Drop me a line to the Bedford, Covent Garden, and tell your husband he's not to fidget about wine ; I am peculiar in that respect, and my own wine-merchant will send down wnat is good for me, or at all events what I take. If you can't take me m. get me comfortable lodgings near, and, upon second thoughts, perhaps that would be best, though I should like to dine, &c. with you for the sake of your society. You have a baby, you know, and the most estimable babies will give vent to screams and wailings, which no bachelor, much less an old one, appreciates.

"Kind regards to your husband.

"Ever, dear Bessie,

"Your affectionate Uncle,

"JOHN MADINGLEY."

"We can't well take him in, Maurice. He will require a couple of rooms to make him thoroughly comfortable; besides, I should be on tenterhooks every time —— "

"Baby lifted up his voice and wept," interposed Maurice, laughing, "and it is not to be supposed that young autocrat is going to change his habits to accommodate a great uncle. No. No, Bessie, I'll get a comfortable bedroom and sitting-room

E 2

at Bevan's close by. He can lunch, dine, and
spend as much of the evening as he chooses
with us, and will have his own rooms to re-
treat to whenever he wants to be quiet. It
will all work very well, only, little woman,
don't spare the table money while Uncle
John's with us."

"Never fear," replied Bessie, merrily, "we
will go in for riotous living, which will probably throw out his gout, and bring down a
solemn anathema on your devoted head.
Who is your other letter from ?"

"This," said Bessie, as she tore it open,
"is from the Bridge Court people. They
really are very kind—read it——"

"DEAR MRS. ENDERBY,

"Will you both come and spend next
week with us? Your husband's old friend
Mr. Grafton has promised to pay us a visit,
and I am sure will enjoy a talk over old
days with him. Pray tell Mr. Enderby I

can take no refusal. If his duties require his presence in Tunnleton, he can walk over after breakfast, and be out again easily in time for dinner. I guarantee that his days shall be at his own disposal if necessary.

" With kindest regards from both myself and the girls, believe me,

" Sincerely yours,

" LOUISA BALDERS."

" Bridge Court, Tuesday.

"P.S. Let us know when I am to send the carriage for you on Monday."

" It is very kind of them, and would be a very pleasant change, I should like it immensely, but I suppose it cannot be managed," said Bessie.

" Why not ? " rejoined her husband.

" Well, you see, Uncle John is coming; it is impossible we can go away for a week under those circumstances."

" Nonsense! this is for next week; Uncle John is not coming until the week after Goodwood—three weeks hence. No, it will all fit in very well, write and say we shall be delighted to come; as Mrs. Balders said, I can easily walk over and do my work."

" But who is your letter from, Maurice ? " replied Bessie.

"Oh, I had quite forgotten all about that. In the excitement produced by Uncle John's determination to visit Tunnleton, I might well forget everything else; you seem to forget that I have never seen this mysterious uncle, who, like the uncle of the old comedies or the beneficent genii of fairy tales, showers his gold upon us. My letter? why it's from Bob Grafton; let's see what he has got to say. '

" 46, Half-Moon Street.

" DEAR MAURICE,

" No end of congratulations on the result

of the Chesterfields. Mr. Brook, there is no
doubt, possesses a real clinker in the 'Wandering Nun.' I remember a wily old racing
man once said to me, ' There is no much
better chance for a backer of horses than the
getting knowledge of a good two-year old
and following it steadily all through the
season. Now that is exactly your position.
You are following what I firmly believe to
be the best two-year old we have seen, with
the additional advantage of not risking a
shilling."

" I wish Mr. Grafton wouldn't write in
that manner," interposed Bessie.

" Don't interrupt," rejoined her husband.

" John Madingley's was an eccentric
wedding present, but on my word it promises
to turn out a very profitable one, and a very
useful one, no doubt in these early days of
your career, when a few extra hundreds
naturally come in handy. The Ham Stakes

at Goodwood lie at her mercy, and I can't see what is to beat her in "the Champagnes" at Doncaster, and to wind up with she has several engagements in the October meetings at Newmarket, though what she will be slipped for one can't tell at present. She is likely anyway to prove a veritable gold-mine to Messrs. Enderby and Brook. I was going to volunteer myself as a visitor for a night or two next week, but I have had a letter from Mrs. Balders asking me to Bridge Court, and assuring me that I should meet you both; so we will have our gossip there, and I will describe the 'Nun' to you. She takes after her sire, and gallops like a piece of machinery.

"Good-bye for the present. Trusting to see you next week, and with kind regards to Mrs. Enderby, believe me ever yours,

"ROBERT GRAFTON."

"I shall be very pleased to meet Mr

Grafton again," said Bessie, " but Maurice, dear, don't be angry if I give one word of caution. I know you will have some racing talk with Mr. Grafton ; but please don't talk about it in public. You know what a scandal is already raised here, and, though the Bridge Court people are not so particular, yet it is wonderful how things get round, and it really is calculated to do you harm in your profession."

Maurice made no reply. " Do him harm in his profession!" Suddenly it flashed across him whether he had not made a mistake ; whether he could ever be fitted for the high office he had taken on himself ; or whether it would not be better to pause before seeking to be ordained priest.

CHAPTER IV.

BITTEN OF THE TARANTULA.

HAVING read the papers, and pronounced his views on the political situation in those grave sonorous tones to which the club morning-room was so well accustomed, General Maddox shouldered his white umbrella, and made his way home to luncheon. He saw as he entered his dining-room that Mrs. Maddox was evidently in what he termed a state of fuss.

"General," she exclaimed, "I have had

one of the Torkesly girls here this morning, and you will hardly believe it when I tell you, that, in spite of all that has passed, the Enderbys have actually gone to stay at Bridge Court."

"No, you don't mean it!" ejaculated the general, for once surprised out of his customary phlegmatic manner.

"Indeed, I do; Clara Torkesly saw it with her own eyes. Saw them get into a Bridge Court carriage at their own door, and drive off with the boxes' and portmanteaus outside."

"It is very odd what made the Balders take them up," said the general, meditatively.

"I presume you will think it your duty to interfere?" remarked the lady sharply.

"Me! interfere?" said the general; "why how can I interfere?"

"I presume you will write to Mr. Balders

and explain to him that he is entertaining
a gambling clergyman who ought to be
unfrocked ---- "

" Nonsense! I haven't met Mr. Balders
half-a-dozen times altogether, and our acquaintance is of the very slightest. I can't
interfere about whom he may think proper
to entertain at Bridge Court; but my
opinion is unchanged about Mr. Enderby,
and I shall certainly recommend all my
friends in Tumnleton to keep clear of him."

" I contend, general, if you did your
duty you would write to Mr. Balders at
once."

" Then for once, my dear, I shall not do
my duty. I am not going to run the risk
of being snubbed for such uncalled-for interference in an almost stranger's affairs as
that would be. When I conceive I am
entitled to speak I shall do so."

" And I tell you, general, you're not only

entitled to speak now, but you're not doing duty by society if you do not," retorted Mrs. Maddox, with all the obstinacy and steady adherence to her point that a vindictive woman usually displays under such circumstances. Mrs. Maddox was quite conscious that she had had the worst of her skirmish with Mrs. Enderby. It was more bitter than the case of those, who, seeking wool, come home shorn. She had gone forth to patronize and came back "snubbed." There was no other word for it, and when that happens to any of us, reprisals, if they cannot be made on the offender, must be made upon somebody else. Do not the veracious legends of the House of Ingoldsby remind us how a great warrior of the Louis Quatorze times

> " Had just tickled the tail of Field-marshal Turenne,
> Since which the Field-marshal's most pressing concern
> Was to tickle some other chief's tail in his turn."

Mrs. Maddox could not retaliate directly upon Bessie, but she could through her husband, and she meant to do so.

Before the general could reply the door opened and the man-servant said, " Mr. Jarrow is in the drawing-room, and says he is particularly anxious to see you, sir."

" Say I will be with him immediately, Williams. Now what can Jarrow want? I should think he has come to admit that he can defend Mr. Enderby no longer."

When the general entered his drawing-room, he found Mr. Jarrow distended with importance on the hearth-rug. Now the general was pompous in his manner, but if there was one man who, so to speak, " over-flowed and drowned him " in this particular it was the rector of St. Mary's. The Reverend Jacob Jarrow was continually, when upon his travels, mistaken for a high ecclesiastic in consequence of his extremely patronizing, condescending manner, and General Maddox had always an uncomfortable feeling of being defeated at his own game when thrown, as had happened more than once, into collision with the rector. There was nothing much in either man in reality. Both depended upon this imposing grandeur of manner—and that proving ineffective had nothing left but to retire from the fray discomfited. But the credulity of mankind is such that they were wont to be regarded as distinguished members of their respective professions, although their records afforded no grounds for such belief.

"Good morning, Mr. Jarrow," said the general, as he entered the room. "Charmed to see you, as the servant told me you had something particular to say. I am afraid I owe this visit more to business than sociability."

"Yes, general," returned the rector, "it

is my duty as one of her principal sons in
Tumleton to repel all attacks made against
the Church. Sir, you ventured to bring a
charge against my curate, which, had it been
true, would have amounted in my eyes to
immorality in a minor degree. I have inquired into that charge, and find it to be
utterly false. I call upon you now to retract it, and to express regret that you
should ever have permitted yourself to have
made it."

The general drew himself up to his full
height before he replied, then he said slowly
but firmly :

" I regret to say, Mr. Jarrow, that I can
do nothing of the kind. What evidence
have you of Mr. Enderby's innocence ?
Nothing, I presume, but his own word. The
bare denial of the accused hardly holds
good in a court of justice. I have sat upon
court martials in my time."

"The decision of which," interposed Mr. Jarrow, pompously, "I'm given to understand is usually in defiance of all evidence"

"You are speaking, Mr. Jarrow," said the general, flushing slightly, "of a court of which you have no knowledge. The accumulation of evidence against Mr. Enderby is very strong. He has been perpetually discussing racing for some time past. He takes an extraordinary interest in a particular race; shows a feverish interest to know the result of it, and, whereas before that race he had been—I am told—in difficulties about money matters, he displays great command of that essential a few days afterwards, and finally lodges a good round sum to his credit at the bank."

"Then, General Maddox, I am to understand that you decline to withdraw the accusation you have made?"

"Certainly I do," replied the general, " until I am convinced it is unfounded."

"And that, sir," said Mr. Jarrow, swelling like an outraged turkey-cock, "you will speedily be convinced of in a court of law if Enderby follows my advice. How you have picked up all this information about his private affairs I don't pretend to conjecture, but it displays a curiosity about your neighbours' affairs which I should hardly give you credit for taking. If Enderby follows my advice he will bring an action for libel against you. Good morning, General Maddox!" and Mr. Jarrow fumed out of the room.

The general felt not a little discomfited. He felt as unforgiving as ever towards Maurice Enderby, and moreover he still firmly believed that he was guilty of the charge preferred against him, and only aggravated his offence by solemnly denying it, but he was conscious that he had had considerably the worst of the argument with the rector. That taunt about prying into his neighbours' affairs had gone severely home to him. It was not the man's nature to do so, but the idle gossiping life of an inland watering-place eats into the bones, gets into the blood. Life is so circumscribed that we take an unnatural interest in the doings of those around us. He did not much believe in any action for libel being brought against him, although he was fain to confess it would be doosid unpleasant if such a thing did take place. He could see already from the final taunt that Mr. Jarrow had thrown out that a sharp cross-examining barrister could at all events give him a very unpleasant half-hour in the witness-box.

At this juncture he was joined by his wife, and no sooner was that lady made acquainted with the object of Mr. Jarrow's

visit than she at once proclaimed no sur-
render, and expressed her intention of
nailing her colours to the mast.

"Mr. Jarrow, indeed! A pompous, med-
dling priest, who, upon the strength of having
written some stupid bombastic letters in the
local journals, believed himself a literary
man and a great controversialist. Pooh!
a fig for the Rev. Jacob Jarrow! He was
always fussing about something! Let him
fuss about this, and if Mr. Enderby was fool
enough to listen to him he would see what
good he got out of it. If Mr. Enderby chose
to invite the public to inspect the quagmires
of his career he could do so; wiser men
boarded them over and kept silence about
them."

Maurice and his wife, meanwhile, were
thoroughly enjoying their stay at Bridge
Court. The rector, with all his failings,
was a good-natured man, and had conceived

a real liking for his new curate, and, hearing where Maurice was going, he at once proposed to take a considerable portion of his, Maurice's, duties off his hands for that week, so that he was left pretty much his own master at Bridge Court.

Bessie thoroughly revelled in the complete freedom from all household affairs, and enjoyed the fruit, the lounging in the grounds, and the lawn-tennis. The Miss Balders, too, thoroughly frank, unaffected English girls, made a great deal of her, and she got on capitally with them, while, to Maurice, chattering over old times or things generally with his friend Bob Grafton, was a quiet luxury which he fully appreciated.

" It's a rum start, old John Madingley's coming down to Tunnleton," said Grafton, one evening in the smoking-room ; " you've never met him, you say ; well, it is good

you should do so, and whoever recommended
him to nurse his gout here did you a good
turn."

"Yes; but there is one very singular
thing about it. He writes to me to get
lodgings for him close to my own house, and
proposes to live with us. Now Richard
Madingley, his heir, has taken a house in
Tunnleton and entertains a good deal. He
has a very nice house, and could have put
his relation up without any trouble.
Curious rather he didn't write to him,
isn't it ? "

"Yes; I never heard of Richard Madingley, and I never heard where John Madingley's money was likely to go, but, though
he's a wonderful hale, hearty man for his
seventy years, that last is a question that
we shall probably have answered for us
before long," said Bob, musingly ; " so the
fellow gives out that he is heir to Bingwell ?

He must have done or the people here could never have arrived at such knowledge."

" Yes, it is owing to his own volunteered information on the subject that Tunnleton is aware of the fact. My wife never heard of him any more than you, but she owns to being very hazy about her cousins generally. She lost her father when she was young and has never known much about his family, with the exception of Uncle John, the elder of the brothers."

Grafton looked up suddenly and said, although in careless tones,

" Does this newcomer know your wife is a Madingley ? "

"I should think not; but, Bob, I want to speak to you about something else; I am afraid I have made a grave mistake in the profession I have selected. I begin to think I am not fitted for clerical life."

" Can't say I ever thought you were,"

rejoined Grafton sententiously, as he emitted a cloud of tobacco from under his moustache, " you ride too straight and are too fond of sport generally to sober down into a parson of these days. Forty or even thirty years ago you might have done, but you're too late, my boy."

" Why didn't you tell me so before ?" said Maurice, somewhat bitterly.

" My dear fellow, what business had I to intrude such advice upon you ? It is one of those things a man must think out for himself."

" I don't know what to do, but I think I shall throw it up."

" Well," said Bob, " you're not ordained priest as yet, and therefore you have plenty of time to think the matter over. Now I'm going to volunteer my advice. Your chance has come to you : think it seriously over, and when your mind is clearly made up

unbosom yourself to John Madingley. He's
in great spirits just now at the running of
his pet filly, is evidently very kindly disposed to your wife, and, I should think,
would be disposed to assist you in any
career you may determine to embark on;
only remember, make up your mind and
know what you want him to help you in.
You can't be such a fool as to think of the
turf."

"No," rejoined Maurice; "I'll admit
Uncle John's legacy has made me think
much more about it than I ever did previously, and I, in my dismay upon finding
how absorbed I was getting in its doings,
on one occasion actually pictured myself as
perpetrating that folly, but I need scarcely
say that is by no means my view of 'a
career.' I sometimes think Uncle John's
wedding present has been a very dubious
benefit."

Grafton looked at his friend for a few seconds with no little astonishment, and then, with a shrug of the shoulders, rejoined quietly,

" Well, it's a dubious benefit I only wish some one would confer upon *me*. My dear Maurice, don't build upon it, but without your bothering your head about it, your wife's eccentric present ought, in the course of this year, and the next, if you have any luck, to be worth not hundreds, but some few thousands, to you, a comfortable send-off in any new line you may strike out."

" You are right, old man," rejoined Maurice, " I shall follow your advice to the letter. I shall think well over what I am going to do, and put racing away from my mind as much as possible. By-the - way, I think you said the Ham

Stakes at Goodwood was the next event the Wandering Nun started for?"

A tremendous guffaw from Bob Grafton roused Maurice to a sense of the absurdity of the question on the top of his previous protestation. It was well the pair had the smoking-room to themselves that night or the room would have rung with laughter.

"Hold me! hold me!" exclaimed Bob, as soon as he could control his merriment, "if ever there was a man badly bitten by the turf tarantula, you are the party. Bless you, I can understand it, I have dabbled in it all my life; used to bet in saveloys and pounds of raisins when I was a small boy. The complaint's old and chronic with me, but you have got all the early and inflammatory symptoms."

"Nonsense, Bob. I'll admit being be-witched by the 'Nun.' I told you the present was a dubious benefit; but don't think I mean to carry my racing experiences further; however, after such a piece of inconsistency as I have just been guilty of, I don't think I can do better than be off to bed."

"Good night," rejoined Grafton; "if you think a laugh will do Mrs. Enderby good before going to sleep you had better recount that speech to her. I shall just finish my cigar and then follow your example."

"He is right about one thing," mused Grafton, as he smoked on after Maurice had left the room; "he is not fit for a parson, and what the deuce he is to turn his hand to I don't know. I fancy he would have made a good soldier, but I suppose the time has gone by for that; I'm afraid he is too old."

CHAPTER V.

THE WIRE FROM GOODWOOD.

But the stereotyed parson's week came to an end, and the Saturday saw Maurice and his wife back in their little house at Tunnleton. Bob Grafton, in a spirit of sheer good nature, volunteered to telegraph in order to assuage that feverish curiosity which Maurice admitted feeling when he knew that Mr. Madingley's flying filly was to run.

"Now, don't you go fidgeting about, I

shall be at Goodwood, and will send you a
wire from the course. Don't you go into
the club to look at the tissue, you shall
have the news before they get it there, you
bet. Good-bye, Mrs. Enderby, don't let
your husband read sporting intelligence,
and give him a dose of chloral whenever he
manifests a proclivity to talk racing."

Bessie laughed as she stretched out her
hand to say good-bye, but it was rather an
anxious little laugh all the same, for she was
seriously uneasy about this unfortunate interest which her husband took in the affair.

They were destined to have speedy evidence of what Mr. Jarrow's partizanship
brought upon them. General Maddox, rather
appalled by the fierce front displayed by the
rector of St. Mary's, had strolled discon-
solately off to confer with his great friend
General Praun, and that irascible warrior,
who was as hot, not as an *Indian*, but as an

English curry, at once took the fierce and furious view that might have been expected of him.

" Bring an action of libel ! He should like to see Jarrow bring one ! he should like to see Enderby bring one ! upon the whole it would seem that he preferred all Tunnleton should bring actions for libel ! He would teach them he was not to be bullied. He had met traders in India under the guise of missionaries, and had never failed to denounce them. He had met a betting man in Tunnleton under the guise of a parson, and he *had* denounced him. He had never been afraid of doing his duty, and wasn't going to flinch from doing it now. Let them bring their actions for libel ! let them put him in the box and listen to what he had to tell them, Messrs. Jarrow and Enderby would be very sorry in half-an-hour that they had invited his revelations ! "

A great man Praun no doubt; had gone through life under this delusion, and been accepted as such by numbers of his acquaintance, chiefly on account of an irritable temper and natural combativeness. But he was no judge of what constituted evidence! and what he termed his revelations would have been pronounced mere hearsay and gossip and no evidence at all by a court of law.

Now the next week was Goodwood, and, do what he would, Maurice could not abstain from further glances at the sporting intelligence in his own daily paper. It is useless to rail against the infirmity of human nature, but it is scarce in accordance with our common frailty not to manifest curiosity of what may be the result of a lottery or raffle in which we have taken tickets. Still Maurice manfully refrained from entering the club, or throwing himself in the way of its sporting frequenters. He contented himself with slowly gathering the news of the Goodwood doings in his paper next morning; but on the Wednesday afternoon came an end to this. Between four and five a boy arrived with the yellow tissue, and it need scarcely be said that a Miss Torkesly happened to be passing and witnessed its delivery. The telegram was of the briefest, it was simply this—

"Congratulations! the Wandering Nun won easily by a length.— R. GRAFTON. Goodwood Racecourse."

A thrill of exultation ran through Maurice's veins. It is no use disputing it! To nine hundred and ninty-nine men out of a thousand the acquisition of money *is* inspiriting, let their profession be what it may. Maurice did not know exactly what the winning of the Ham Stakes meant, but he had little doubt that it represented two or three hundred to his credit at his banker's.

He sat with the telegram in his hand, musing over several little things in the way of furnishing that Bessie wanted. He thought also of that pony-carriage of which they had indulged in hazy dreams; a pony-carriage with its etceteras that they had pictured as coming within their reach, when editors should at length awaken to a proper sense of the value of his—Maurice's— contributions; and here was this money coming in without his lifting a finger (so he admitted with a half sense of shame) to earn it. Granting he was a popular contributor, Maurice could not but think how many articles he must need write, how many weary hours he must need pass at his writing-table, before he could hope to make that sum of money! It was demoralising— he knew it was. He was conscious that, despite all his struggles to the contrary, he was becoming to all intents and purposes a gambler. He did not *actually* play, he did not *actually* bet; but, for all that, he was watching the racing reports as men do the spinning of the ball or the fall of the card at Monte Carlo. However he soon shook off his reverie; none of us wax solemn for long over the winning of money, more especially won from neither friend nor acquaintance, and it was with quite a gay countenance that he left his study and ascended to his wife's drawing-room.

" Well, Bessie," he exclaimed, " I have just had a telegram from Grafton to say that your uncle's filly is victorious again. I really am glad that he is coming to us next week. He cannot surely mean to keep on presenting us with hundreds. When he good-naturedly said that you were to go halves with him in what the ' Nun ' might

win, he probably thought she might pick up
one decent stake, but could hardly have supposed that he was the owner of the very best
two-year-old of the season—a filly whose
winnings are likely to be computed by thousands."

"No, no," rejoined Bessie, "I agree with
you, I don't think that could have been his
intention; but Uncle John is a man of his
word, and sure to stick to it. Still his
coming here will give you an excellent opportunity to release him for what he has
already done; and tell him we really expect
to participate no further in the Wandering
Nun's successes."

"You are quite right; I have got a capi-
tal first floor for him just over the way, and
as soon as he has settled down I'll explain
this to him. He has been very loyal to his
promise; many men would have considered

a cheque for a hundred quite sufficient redemption of such a pledge."

" He has been very good to us, Maurice. I am no purist, as you know, but Uncle John's present to some extent represents dabbling in the turf. I know, dear, you don't actually, but morally it is otherwise. We will thank Uncle John and have done with it."

Maurice stirred his tea and quietly assented to his wife's proposition. He meant it thoroughly; he wished to disentangle himself from the meshes of the turf; but the abandoning that fascination, except under compulsion, requires rigid resolution, as many a moth who has scorched his wings past redemption at the fatal candle has sadly owned, through many succeeding years of exile or poverty. To Maurice it was so easy to continue his interest in it; he could always calm his conscience with the assurance that he never actually staked money on the result, but the excitement of watching what to him was really speculation on its chances was one he would be somewhat loth to forego when it came to the point.

Mr. Richard Madingley had given a great garden-party, which was followed up by a dance in honour of his engagement. The greater part of Tunnleton society was present at this *fête*, and the Enderby scandal, as it had come to be called, was a prominent topic of discussion. The adverse party were much in the ascendant, indeed Maurice could count few friends in that assembly, but he had one powerful one in the person of the Reverend Jacob Jarrow, who had no idea of a curate of his being found fault with by any one but himself.

Mr. Jarrow was a person formidable to combat; his very failings tended to make him an awkward antagonist; his pomposity, self-complacency, and obstinacy were hard to contend with. You can't convince a man who starts with a steady determination that he will not be convinced; ridicule he was impervious to, and, in the matter of words, both ponderous and voluminous; you could no more have talked the Reverend Mr. Jarrow down than his church steeple.

General Maddox, after his last week's experience, kept clear of him, but the irascible Praun could not refrain from dashing in to rescue his wife from a pretty sharp lecture on want of charity towards her neighbours, which, without exactly mentioning Maurice's name, evidently had his story for its text.

"It's all very well, Mr. Jarrow; we all know that you consider a curate of yours can do no wrong; that you decline even to listen to the evidence against him; but you can hardly expect that the unsupported

word of the rector of St. Mary's will white-
wash Mr. Enderby in the eyes of men of
the world. I'm told that you counsel him
to bring an action for libel against some of
us; I can only say, let him, let him, sir, as
far as I am personally concerned; he will
find that more complete exposure is all he
will take by that move !"

"I have not only counselled him to do
so, but I shall urge him still more strongly
to persist in such resolution. People who
calumniate their fellow-creatures find themselves mulcted in serious damages in these
days; you will perhaps discover, general,
that mere statement doesn't constitute
evidence," and with this the rector walked
away, with the air of a man who has completely crushed his opponent, most madden-
ing to witness.

"Evidence, forsooth !" exclaimed the
enraged general to his wife; "the idea of

any parson telling *me*, a man that has sat on hundreds of court-martials, that I don't know what evidence is!" and then the general walked off, fuming and muttering, I am afraid, words not altogether complimentary to the clerical profession generally, but he was soon destined to receive consolation, and, ere he had gone far, he came across his host, who was being excitedly appealed to by some of his fair guests on the subject of Maurice's iniquities.

"You see, you know all about these things, Mr. Madingley; you oughtn't to, and of course you'll give it up when you're married, but you really should be a judge of whether Mr. Enderby really is guilty of gambling."

Dick Madingley, who was by nature relentless in his vengeance, had steadily adhered to his *rôle* of Iago. He had nothing to say to it; he knew nothing about it; it was no affair of his, but, if you asked him as a man of the world—well, Mr. Enderby had endeavoured to make the most of his information.

" Ah, I am afraid so. It is very sad that a clergyman should give way to such madness," observed Angelina Torkesly, with a deep sigh; " but after what I saw yesterday I am afraid there can be no doubt that Mr. Enderby has yielded to temptation."

And then the fair Angelina, in all the glory of contributing a fresh sauce to the highly-spiced dish of gossip they were discussing, narrated her story of the yellow envelope and the telegraph boy.

Dick Madingley said nothing, but in the eyes of the audience this evidently was an important fact that admitted of no rebutting, and they were expressing their opinion to that effect freely when an unctuous voice boomed upon their ears.

" I would recommend you to be a little more reticent of your opinions, my good people. This accusation is about to become the subject of an action for libel, in which one or two of the leading personages of Tunnleton will figure prominently, and several more have the privilege of entering the witness-box."

A sudden shower could not have more effectually washed out the conversation than the rector's announcement. It was the first society had heard of such a thing as an action for libel being contemplated, and society had a hazy idea of the pains and penalties connected with that style of prosecution, but Tunnleton was prompt to recognise that it was a very unpleasant affair to be mixed up in. The Reverend Jacob Jarrow had taken up the cudgels with such good will for his curate, that he had quite persuaded himself that this action

should be and would be brought, although
Maurice had never for one moment hinted
at such a course. However, his speech had
the effect of dispersing the little knot, and
Mr. Jarrow found himself left face to face
with his host and with General Praun as
the sole auditor of what might pass between
them.

"It is very good of you to stand up for
your curate, Mr. Jarrow," remarked Dick
Madingley, suavely, "but, if you have any
influence with him, you had best counsel
him to drop this action for libel. He is no
friend of mine or you would see him here to-
day, but I don't like to see a man make a
fool of himself. I'm the last fellow to find
fault with any one for having sporting tastes,
but if a man does have a little flutter over a
race it's no use telling lies about it. I don't
pretend to be a censor of morals at my time
of life, but, Mr. Jarrow, if it is wrong for a

parson to bet, I can't see that he mends things by denying his having done so."

"You had better be very careful how you reiterate that calumny," said Mr. Jarrow, pompously.

"Had I," replied Dick Madingley, with an evil gleam in his light blue eyes, "Good! next time you see your model-assistant, just ask him this question: Did the telegraph bring you good news from Goodwood on Wednesday?"

"Good gracious, what do mean?" exclaimed Mr. Jarrow.

"Nothing more than I say. Simply ask Mr. Enderby if the telegraph brought him good news from Goodwood on Wednesday. If his answer satisfies you I am willing to retract my recently expressed opinion."

It was a bold coup on Richard Madingley's part, for telegrams refer to many other things than racing, and Dick had no idea

of what Enderby's telegraph was about
really. Still he knew that it was the Goodwood week, and had managed to wring from
the telegraph clerk, with whom he was on intimate terms, that it did come from the
ducal gathering.

As for the Reverend Mr. Jarrow he was
fairly taken aback, and left, to use nautical
parlance " in irons," and ere he could recover himself his host was gone.

CHAPTER VI.

JOHN MADINGLEY.

EARLY in the following week John Madingley arrived in Tunnleton. There had been
no flourish of trumpets announcing his
arrival, the Enderbys had mentioned it
to no one, and the quiet, countrified, old-
fashioned clergyman who stepped into the
very - well - known lodgings that Maurice
had secured for him attracted no attention
in the first instance. But in a few days
Tunnleton awoke to the fact that Mrs.

Enderby had got an uncle who had arrived within its gates, and that the name of that uncle was Madingley, and then the gossiping little town literally ran wild with boundless conjecture. What relation was the new-comer to Mr. Richard? How extremely odd, if he was a relation, that Mr. Richard had never alluded to his expected arrival, and then Tunnleton remembered that Richard Madingley had run up to town, on some lawyer's business it was said, and presumably connected with the marriage settlement.

Tunnleton felt mystified, and if there is one thing a provincial town invariably resents and places the worst construction on it is this. An uncle of Mrs. Enderby, then why did the Enderbys keep his approaching advent a secret? Mr. Enderby's ways apparently, like those of "the Heathen Chinee," were peculiar, and once more

society shook its head over Maurice's iniquities and came to the conclusion, that, as
far as Richard Madingley was concerned,
despite the uncommonness of the name, they
were namesakes but not relatives.

However there were two people in Tumleton who did not accept this view of things.
Mr. Molecombe the banker, whose daughter
was betrothed to Dick Madingley, thought it
behoved him to call at all events on one who
might prove to be a somewhat important
relative of his future son-in-law, and, to say
the truth, was not quite so well satisfied in
the matter of settlements as a staid business-
man should be before he surrendered his
daughter to a comparative stranger. Mr.
Molecombe came to the grave resolution that
he would call. He had sounded his junior
partner Frank Chylton pretty severely on
this point, but Frank was so indignant at
the omission of the Enderbys from the

Molecombe garden-party of some few weeks
ago, that he steadfastly withheld the information he possessed, and there was growing
up gradually in Frank Chylton's mind a
doubt as to whether Richard Madingley was
quite what he professed to be. He had
never even hinted such a thing to Maurice,
but it struck him as curious that Richard
Madingley seemed quite unaware that Mrs.
Enderby's maiden name had been identical
with his own, and that she was a niece of the
man whose property he professed himself
heir to. It had occurred to him of late that
Mr. Richard Madingley was perhaps drawing on his imagination when he described
himself as heir to that Yorkshire property,
and that the succession to it might be more
matter of hope than a declared intention on
the part of the present proprietor.

The Reverend John Madingley of Bingwell might be a pronounced fact in his own

country and in many other places, but in
Tunnleton he had been a mere impalpable
shadow in which they took no sort of interest till the arrival of his reputed heir, and
even then that Mrs. Enderby was also a
relation of the Yorkshire squire and rector
had been quite forgotten by the few people
who had known it, with the exception of
the Chyltons.

Mr. Molecombe in due course presented
himself at John Madingley's lodgings, and,
in response to the conventional "not at
home," desired to see that gentleman's valet,
and explained to him that he did not come
within the catalogue of ordinary visitors, as
his daughter was engaged to be married to
Mr. Richard Madingley.

The valet's face was immoveable, and his
manner most deferential as he listened to
the banker's story, but he firmly though
politely reiterated that his orders were im-

perative, that his master was in delicate health, and regretted that he was unable to receive visitors.

Mr Molecombe retired considerably disappointed. He thought, considering the circumstances, the rector of Bingwell might have made an effort to see him.

There is a great resemblance between humanity and sheep. Despite their first impressions, no sooner was Tunnleton aware that Mr. Molecombe had called, than it occurred to several of the prominent members of Tunnleton society, who had profited by Richard Madingley's hospitality, that it would be perhaps advisable to call upon the new comer. Mr. Molecombe had, of course, satisfied himself of the relationship before committing himself in this wise. But the same answer was invariably returned which had met the banker on his visit—" Delicate

health, and deeply regretted he was unable
to receive visitors."

Not reckoning the Enderbys, John Madingley made but one exception to this rule,
and that, to the unfeigned astonishment of
Tunmleton, was General Shrewster. That
he was a self-contained man, and not given
to slopping over like a full pail when jogged
against, his acquaintance were aware. Still
it is very odd that he had never mentioned
his acquaintance with the master of Bingwell, whom he must evidently know intimately or he would scarcely have been
admitted when he called.

It was quite true, General Shrewster,
although near a score of years younger than
John Madingley, had been a contemporary
of his upon the turf. It was many a year
ago since the general had abandoned that
fascinating pursuit, but there were plenty of
old race-goers even now who could recollect

how Captain Shrewster used to "shake the
ring." How he would dash in at the last
moment, in the days when men really did
bet, and write down three or four pages of
his betting-book in about the same time as
it has taken the writer to scrawl this para-
graph. "It's a treat," an old trainer once
remarked, "to put the Captain on a good
thing, he's the pluckiest bettor I ever saw!
and when he goes in he fairly makes the
ring dazed before he snaps his betting-book
to again. He has had them so often and so
heavily, they are a bit cowed now when he
puts down the pieces in earnest."

Yes. General Shrewster's had been the
fate of many another who had started in life
with a good property and plenty of ready
money. How many thousands he had run
through on the turf was a matter only
known to his bankers, and his solicitor. The
large sums that he won by day on the heath

were more than swallowed up by the reckless play he indulged in, at the rooms at
Newmarket, at night. He had wonderful
information and was a most successful specu-
lator, but reckless after-dinner play, at the
gaming table would easily dissipate such
successes, and the gambling houses of
Brighton or the rooms at Doncaster easily
swallowed up the winnings of the ducal
gathering, or successful days on the Town
Moor.

It was in those early days that John
Madingley had known young Shrewster.
It is hardly worth going into, but in
those days the then captain had intimate
relations with the great Northern stable
in which John Madingley trained, and the
rector had been attracted towards him from
the audacity with which he was wont to
back any promising horse of his. They had
become great friends, Shrewster had more

than once been down to stay at Bingwell.
Then came his smash. He had nothing for
it but to exchange to India and leave the
settlement of his affairs to his solicitor. The
result was, a fine fortune became a moderate
competence ; still upon that and his pension
General Shrewster as a bachelor was passing
rich in Tunnleton. He never spoke of his
past, and that complacent little place, which
believed that its knowledge was universal,
was quite unaware that the grey-haired
veteran, who read the morning papers so
placidly, who was never seen in the billiard-
room, and rarely even as a looker-on in the
card-room, was the Captain Shrewster about
whose wondrous turf successes and mad
doings all London had rung a quarter of a
century ago. You may think yourself a big
man, you may flatter yourself that you have
made your mark, but to bring yourself to a
proper sense of the nothingness of all human

ambition there is nothing like a visit to one of those pulseless provincial places. Except you are royalty or the prime minister, there will be slight curiosity regarding you. Swinburne, Wilkie Collins, or Millais, run no risk of being mobbed in such towns.

It was not long before Tunnleton arrived at the fact that General Shrewster was admitted by the recluse of Bevans, as the somewhat ostentatious private hotel where Mr. Madingley had taken up his abode was called, and about this the inquisitive little town marvelled much.

Not an easy man to question, this General Shrewster; could be curt and sarcastic, as more than one social dignitary had discovered, somewhat to his discomfiture. Still, Generals Maddox and Praun, after some talk between themselves, came to the conclusion that Mr. Madingley's eccentric seclusion was a thing to be inquired into, and that the information they sought could only be obtained from General Shrewster. But from this latter the two *gobe-mouches* could extract nothing. General Shrewster told them briefly that he had known John Madingley intimately many years ago, that he had come down to Tunnleton for his health, and was not equal to receiving visitors or making fresh acquaintances.

Even General Praun admitted there was no more to be said; it certainly was open to a man to choose whom he would receive in his own house. Still, as the uncle of Dick Madingley, Tunnleton, he did think, had claims, &c., &c., which only went to prove that "there was no more to be said," by no means, as a rule, closed discussion, there being generally plenty more of inaccurate talk to follow that brief announcement.

Maurice and his wife got on capitally with Uncle John. He looked more like an old-

fashioned country squire than a clergyman,
although his dress was sober enough. He
was generally attired in a single-breasted
pepper-and-salt coat of slightly sporting cut,
drab kerseymere breeches and leggings, and
invariably wore a white scarf of matchless
fold and immaculate purity. He was evidently fond of Bessie, and no sooner did he
discover the fascination the turf had for her
husband than he unfolded the lore of past
decades for his edification, and about the last
fifty years of turf history John Madingley
was a combination of racing calendar and
biographical dictionary very interesting to
listen to for any one whose tastes lay that
way. One thing Maurice remarked as
strange was that he made no allusion to
Richard Madingley, and at first seemed a
little taken aback to find that he was established in Tunnleton; afterwards he appeared
to have heard all about it, but to take very

little interest in Richard or his proceedings.

The following conversation would have created no little excitement in Tunnleton could it have been heard :—

"Good morning, Shrewster! It's very good of you to come and cheer up an old friend who has got very near to the end of his tether. I like a gossip with you over the old times of five and-twenty years ago."

"Yes, Madingley, but it's ended the same way with the lot of us. We plunged and won! We plunged and lost! and the losings always exceeded the winnings by many thousands. My lot was only that of a score of others; you can recollect. You, like a sensible man, raced solely for sport, and when you did bet it was to an extent that never caused you a moment's uneasiness. However, never mind these bygones. I am glad you like young Enderby. He's a good sort."

"Yes, he is!" returned John Madingley. "He is a very good young fellow; but I tell you what, he is in the wrong groove. That chap will never do any good as a parson. They don't stand parsons of my stamp now-a-days, and Maurice is no more fitted for the profession he has chosen than I am, though all the same I have been more conscientious than the world gives me credit for."

"You are quite right," rejoined Shrewster. "Enderby would make a rattling good dragoon, but he will never do any good in his present vocation."

"Well," interposed Mr. Madingley, quickly, "he is not committed to it yet, and he is young enough to change, and I shouldn't mind helping him a little in some other line if he liked."

" And what would your heir say to that?"
inquired General Shrewster, slyly.

John Madingley threw himself back in his
chair, and burst into a roar of laughter.

" Ah," he said at length, " what a com-
motion there will be in Tunnleton when they
come to the rights of that story; in the
course of a few days Scotland Yard will
no doubt have reckoned this gentleman up
for us; but, as I told you before, as for his
being my heir, why I never even heard of
the fellow before. He may have a right to
the name of Madingley, but he is most
assuredly no connection of mine. You tell
me he is engaged to a girl in this town, a
daughter of that banker fellow who called
upon me. I don't mean to see him, but I
shall certainly before I leave Tunnleton let
him know that his intended son-in-law is
flying false colours. But in the meanwhile,

Shrewster, not a word to any one. I know I can trust you."

" Yes, I know how to keep my tongue between my teeth, and now I'm going to say good bye. You look tired, and will be all the better for a snooze before dinner. Good-bye." And with a warm pressure of the hand the two old friends separated.

CHAPTER VII.

AT THE " BRISTOL " RESTAURANT.

IF there was one man at Tunnleton who
felt uncomfortable about the position of
things it was Mr. Molecombe. His daughter
had heard several times from her *fiancée*,
but Richard Madingley always wound up
by regretting that the well-known dilatory
ways of solicitors still detained him in town.
That was nothing compared to a rebuff he
had received from John Madingley. Not
content with that gentleman's " not at

home," he had thought fit to write to him
to explain Richard Madingley's relation to
his daughter, and the rector of Bingwell's
reply had thrown the banker into a cold
perspiration.   John Madingley had curtly
answered that his health precluded his receiving visitors, and that he had nothing
to say to Richard Madingley's matrimonial
arrangements.

A more uncomfortable answer it was
scarce possible to get from a man who
stood *in loco parentis* to that of a proposed son-in-law.   A second letter elicited
no answer whatever, and, though Mr. Molecombe as yet kept his own counsel, he was
nevertheless seriously discomposed about
the aspect of affairs.   It was a puzzle
beyond his comprehension.   His intended
son-in-law had vanished from Tunnleton
simultaneously with the advent of the relative from whom he professed to expect his

heritage; that might have been accident,
but it was singular that he should not return
nor apparently have been aware of the
Yorkshire rector's coming. Then, again,
John Madingley's note, and the ground he
had apparently taken up, were by no means
reassuring. Elderly gentlemen invariably
expected to be consulted and deferred to
about their heirs' matrimonial intentions,
more especially when such elderly gentlemen's property was entirely at their own
disposal. Mr. Madingley apparently did
not. One solution only of this was possible to the banker's mind, namely, that
the rector of Bingwell most thoroughly
disapproved of the whole affair and intended
to countenance it as little as might be.
This would account for Dick Madingley's
apparent embarrassment about the settlements. There were difficulties probably
between himself and his uncle's lawyers,

for, despite the fact that Richard Madingley had only given himself out as a cousin of the well - known Yorkshire "Squarson." Tunnleton, from the moment they had grasped the fact (rather late in the day) that the owner of Bingwell was to some extent a man of moneyed notability, had insisted on that relationship, and their disgust when this clergyman of the north declined to appear and be worshipped was considerable. Still, let Tunnleton think what it liked, there were two points which there was no getting over. The Reverend John Madingley adhered strictly to his determination to see nobody—while, curiously enough, his relative and heir was apparently unable to return from London. Mr. Molecombe was much too prudent to show any concern about this, but at the same time both he and his family felt extremely uncomfortable about the turn things had taken.

Edith Molecombe, indeed, shrank as far as possible from receiving visitors of any sort. She could say with truth that she heard nearly every other day from her *fiancé*— that his letters were dated from the Bristol Hotel, but that he was still detained in London by those bothering lawyers; all very well this on the surface, but Mr. Molecombe could not but see that within such easy distance from town as Tunnleton was it was very possible for an enamoured young man to run down for a day or so to see his sweetheart, more especially when such an opportunity of presenting his bride-elect to the man who stood to him in place of a father had occurred. It would almost seem as if John Madingley had run down to Tunnleton for that express purpose, and yet Richard seemed to have disappeared as if to controvert it.

Could Mr. Molecombe have looked in at

the Bristol Restaurant one evening, his eyes might not only have been opened, but have been fetched pretty nearly out of his head. Trifling over his dessert with a still unfinished bottle of dry champagne at his right hand, was a slight, wiry, dark-faced, clean-shaven man, allowing himself only the smallest modicum of mutton-chop whisker. A man about whose age it was hopeless to conjecture. He might be either prematurely old or extraordinarily young for his time of life, but he was at all events eating the best hot-house peaches and drinking the best Brut brand the Bristol could furnish, with a *nonchalance* that betokened the most perfect indifference to the amount of his dinner-bill. While he was leisurely picking his teeth, a man clothed in faultless evening attire, with immaculate white tie, who had been apparently so far condescendingly superintending the

other waiters, approached his table with a
deferential bow and said,

" I hope, Mr. Pick, I hope your dinner
has been satisfactory."

" Hallo Dick ! thought you had made
your pile and started something of this kind
on your own account."

" Well, Mr. Pick, I did get a tidy lot
together, and I undoubtedly had a very
good time last year, still I did not think it
quite good enough to cut this place; my
berth here, as you know, is an exceedingly
good one; they are excessively liberal in the
matter of leave, in fact really three days a
week is as much supervision as they demand
from me. I have been in the country a bit
for the benefit of my health."

Mr. Pick received this statement with a
low whistle and a closure of the left eye
that might have been deemed almost insult-
ing by sensitive people.

Richard Madingley continued in the same unmoved tone,

"Things haven't been quite so rosy this season so far; you have always been very good to me, Mr. Pick, and I thought I could rely upon you thoroughly for information about the North Country Stables."

"So you can, Dick, you have always known all I know."

"What about this 'Wandering Nun,' then? You never gave me a hint about *her*, Mr. Pick."

"No," replied the saturnine gentleman irritably. "Dash it, how could I? Those cursed Kilbournes kept the thing so confoundedly dark that there wasn't a soul in the north knew anything about her except perhaps old Madingley and one or two of his cronies. They never let you know, and old Kilburne and his son think a deal before they lay out a pony between 'em, but

they have got a flyer, no mistake about it.
I have learnt it much too late to collar the
loaf ; but you had better follow my lead and
go in for the crumbs."

" My expenses have been very heavy this
season, Mr. Pick."

" *Your* expenses ! " retorted the other
contemptuously, "your expenses be damned !
Look here, Dick Bushman : I promised your
mother to give you a hand, as far as I could,
before she died, and I've done it. I'm not
particular. No man who makes the turf his
vocation can afford to be mealy-mouthed,
but you certainly have no call to heave
rocks at me. I got you your appointment
here, better than that of most clerks in
government offices as far as money and
work goes : I've given you the office whenever I've been in the swim myself, and you
come here whining to me about your expenses and not being advertised of the

Wandering Nun.   D——n it, sir, live on the two pounds a week you will probably command if they turn you off here without a character, and don't trouble me any more!"

" Pray don't mistake me, Mr. Pick. If you would allow me to conduct you to a private room while I explain, and condescend to accept a glass of champagne and a cigar from me, you will be quite satisfied."

" Well, Dick, I could do another pint of 'pop' and a tidy cigar. You ain't a fool, and if you don't rough me up the wrong way I'm good to stand to you still, but that Wandering Nun is a devilish sore subject; there hasn't been such a good thing as that come out of Yorkshire in my time without my knowing all about it : but the Kilburnes, having no real speculators connected with them, had no trouble about keeping this dark ; a few hundreds would represent the investments of Mr. Brooks, his friends and his trainer. But come along and you shall tell me what you've been doing."

Mr. Pick, now a notable member of the ring, had begun life as a footman. The antecedents of the knights of the pencil are mysterious as those of the members of the Stock Exchange; they have their ascension, culmination, and decline, their zenith and their nadir; comet-like they cross the sky and disappear into the obscurity of poverty or sparkle with the temporary effulgence of wealth. Mr. Peck at present gravitated between these points, but he was a philosopher, and, when he could not afford the tariff of the Bristol, was content with a cut off the joint at a luncheon-bar, though, like most of his vocation, he always lived luxuriously when in feather.

Dick led the way to a snug, disengaged dining-room, in which one of his subordinates was already busy manipulating the cork of a champagne bottle.

" Well, I haven't seen much of you lately," remarked Mr. Pick, as he sipped his wine with infinite gusto; " what have you been doing ? "

" I've been doing the swell and setting up as a gentleman of property : never mind where, but not very far from town."

" Yes, you're good at that game, as I know from experience; you can do the pretty and put the side on, Dick, so as to pass for the real article, unless the liquor gets the best of you, and then, like the rest of us, you are apt to display the weaknesses of your past; you've a command of strong language which you're a little disposed to make use of when you're sprung— that's injudicious.   Well, did you have a good time ?   Did you make it pay ? "

" Not quite : but if I could raise a few hun-

dreds more I should have made a good thing
of it. I was fairly established as one of the
swells of the place and engaged to the
daughter of the leading banker there."

" What, you, to a real lady, with
money ? "

" Just so?" rejoined Dick rather sharply ;
"there's nothing very wonderful in that;
I'm not bad-looking, you know ; they all
think I'm comfortably off and that I'm a
gentleman."

The other ejected a cloud of tobacco-
smoke, and then, with a significant wink,
observed,

" Right you are ; a real out-and-outer ;
but you've a past, Master Dick, that respectable people would look upon as somewhat
dubious."

" When the respectable people don't know
it that matters little," replied Dick Madingley ; " but I wanted to see you, and that is

the principal reason that brought me to London."

"Campaign not been profitable as yet, eh?" rejoined Mr. Pick.

"No, but just on the point of becoming so."

"Like 'em all, like 'em all," replied the bookmaker softly. "Like myself, like the beggars who are always on the verge of discovering how to make gold or diamonds, or their fortune. We're always pounded for that other five hundred pounds or so. If we had had that odd hundred or so to plunge with, what a lot of us would be driving in carriages instead of wearing our soles out. The end of your moving history is, you want money and can I find it?"

Dick nodded. He knew his man, and, though Mr. Pick might philosophise himself, words were quite wasted upon him as a matter of business. He would never have

attained the very tolerable turf position he
held had he not been both hard-headed and
practical. The advancing of a little money
where he saw his way to tolerable security,
for exorbitant interest, was quite within his
province.

" You know I have been doing tolerably
well, or you wouldn't see me here ; but you
also know I'm the last man to go into a
speculation blindfold. You'll have to show
your hand, my boy."

" And that is none so easy to do. You
would want to know what the young lady's
fortune was to be."

" Naturally. I've to recover my money
and be liberally recompensed for the accom-
modation," rejoined Mr. Pick gravely.

" That's just the rub. My proposed
father-in-law is somewhat anxious to do the
same thing with regard to myself."

The bookmaker gave vent to a low whistle.

" Under those circumstances," he said, at last, "I think I may say this match won't come off. At all events, it don't sound good enough for this child to risk money on."

" It will come off fast enough if I am not stranded for a few hundreds of ready coin. They all believe down there I'm of a good Yorkshire family, and heir to a nice property."

" A rather credulous population down there, wherever it is," remarked Mr. Pick, with a sneer. " And now, before we go any further, where is it ? "

" Time enough for you to know when you tell me you're good to advance me four or five hundred to carry on the war."

" It is no use, Dick ; when those parliament swells come to the house for supplies, they have to condescend to particulars, and so will you before I part with a ' mag.' "

"I must have the money or chuck the thing up," replied Dick Madingley. "You would have to know it sooner or later, and, as I can't well play the game without a confederate, perhaps the sooner I take you into my confidence the better. I am down at Tunnleton, and living in one of the best bachelor residences in the town."

"I say, isn't that risky? Weren't you afraid of being spotted?"

"No, the Bristol is a little above Tunnleton form, and, as for racing, well, Tunnleton talks a good deal about it, but, bar Epsom, don't know its way to a race-course."

"Any crumbs to be picked up there?" inquired Mr. Pick.

"No; it's not worth while exposing your game at sixpenny pool, nor your knowledge of whist at shilling points—besides it would

have been all against the game I was playing to be counted anything but a fair per-
former in those lines."

" Good, very good ! " remarked the book-
maker.   " There's nothing like understand-
ing when one's little talents are best kept in
the background.   Or else, Dick, amongst
yokels, you're likely to do well at those
amusements."

" Well, you agree with me," replied the
other impatiently ; " fishing for gudgeon is
waste of time when there are salmon in the
pool.   Will you stand to me ? "

" I'll come down and have a look at the
thing, anyway.   You can put me up for a
day or two ? "

" I'll put you up for a week or two, if you
will make up as an old-fashioned sporting
pastor and call yourself my uncle."

" What, the fellow with the property in
Yorkshire ? " exclaimed Mr. Pick.

"That's it. I want you to represent old John Madingley of Bingwell. He's an old man who never goes out of his own county, and they know nothing about him in Tunnleton."

"Never goes out of Yorkshire, don't he? By Heavens, Dick! I saw him at Goodwood last week. The old man came all the way to see his Wandering Nun win the 'Ham.'"

CHAPTER VIII.

MR. MOLECOMBE GETS UNEASY.

Mr. PICK listened to the further evolution of Richard Madingley's scheme with considerable interest, but not altogether with enthusiasm. No man keener than him to turn five hundred pounds into a thousand in a few weeks, and that he computed was about the price he ought to receive for his assistance, pecuniarily and otherwise. But then Mr. Pick had a wholesome dread of placing himself within the clutches of the law, and

he had a vague idea that the personation of
a well-known personage would come under
the head of fraud or conspiracy, or something of that sort.   Moral scruples the
bookmaker had none, still he had escaped
once or twice by the skin of his teeth ; had
indeed once left the dock under the lash of
the judge's tongue, and had to listen to the
regrets of that functionary that his wrong-
doing had been so skilfully planned as to
just defeat the administration of justice.
No, Mr. Pick did not approve of the bill of fare
at Millbank.   No, the bookmaker, although
he had embarked on some very risky enter-
prises in his early career, was too substantial
a man now not to weigh possible results,
however profitable the game might appear
to be, and anything that looked like ending
in a law-court he shrank from.   He was not
quite clear whether the personation of somebody else was not an indictable offence.   He

rather thought it was, he had hazy ideas of " conspiracy with intent to defraud," being a transgression that carried severe pains and penalties. His mouth watered at the idea of the sum he might demand for his help, but he had no idea of burning his fingers in pulling Dick's chestnuts out of the fire.

"I've been thinking this out," he said, slowly, after a silence of some moments, which the other had taken care not to interrupt. " It's rather a risky business, and if I go into it you'll have to pay pretty smartly for my help. I tell you what I'll do. I'll come down and look at it, and that's as much as I'll promise just now. If I fancy the spec. well and good, if not, there's no harm done."

"You will come back with me to-morrow; remember it is important that I should produce the relation from whom I have expectations as soon as may be. I never saw John Madingley, but you have, and well know the sort of line to take up—country parson with sporting tastes."

"I can't personate him to any body who has ever seen him," replied Mr. Pick, "but the chances are nobody in Tunnleton ever has. I'll be ready to-morrow; you wire and order dinner," and, so saying, the book-maker rose to his feet and, nodding good-night, left the room.

Could the precious pair have overheard a conversation at Tunnleton, the going down there would have been deemed inexpedient by both of them.

"No, Madingley, I ran up to town and did what you wished, but you had better, at present, let things take their course. At all events there is nothing to be done with your namesake till he returns. They know nothing about this young gentleman at Scotland Yard, and pooh-poohed the whole business. Said that he very likely had a

right to the name, and had only exag-
gerated in claiming relationship with you.
In short," concluded General Shrewster,
" they decline to interfere at present in any
way, and I suppose they're right. This
fellow would probably declare he only
claimed to be a distant connection of yours,
and that the rest was merely Tunnleton
gossip."

"Yes," replied John Madingley, "it is
always open to a man to claim that sort of
kinship, and he does himself little harm
even if the other side disavow it."

" Yes, a cool hand like this young gentleman will get out of it easily enough. He
does not want money apparently, and is
certainly not deficient in cheek."

" I know the sort," rejoined Madingley,
laughing, " plenty of bounce and swagger
till they're collared. We'll leave the fellow
alone, and only give Mr. Molecombe a hint

in case his daughter's marriage with my
namesake becomes imminent. It will be
for him then to discover whether Mr.
Richard Madingley is sailing under false
colours or not."

" Yes," replied Shrewster, with a quiet
smile," and it will be a terrible shock to
Tunnleton should he turn out to be a rank
impostor."

" Yes," rejoined the master of Bingwell,
" the idea that he has been regularly had
rouses the bile of the Yorkshireman, and I
don't suppose the southerners take it more
kindly."

So, it having been settled between them
that for the present they would merely
watch the course of events, neither John
Madingley nor his old friend troubled themselves any more for the present about the
doings of this new star that had suddenly
risen above the town horizon.

But if they did not trouble themselves about Dick Madingley's proceedings Tunnleton did; and the Prauns and the Maddoxes and the Torkeslys shook their heads, and agreed that there was something excessively odd in the newly-engaged man's persistent absence. Mr. Pick had suddenly found that his own legitimate business would detain him some time longer in London, and with the somewhat hazardous game that Richard Madingley was playing he did not consider it advisable to re-appear upon the scene until his pockets were replenished. On that point Mr. Pick was very decided— he would advance no money until, as he expressed it, he had been "to look at the speculation."

Mrs. Maddox said boldly that the young men had changed a good deal since her time; that if Maddox had treated her in such *nonchalant* fashion after they were engaged he would very soon have "had the mitten."

Mrs. Praun opined that there was no standing the youth of the present day, they really seemed to expect the young ladies to do all the love-making, to which her irascible husband responded, "And by gad, madam, they are not disappointed," which produced one of those Mediterranean squalls wont to disturb the even tenour of the Prauns' domestic life — a hot-tempered couple who not only indulged in volcanic explosions at home but combined in volcanic irruptions abroad, and were a terror and—metaphorically—a very lava-flood to any weak-kneed society they might get into. As for the Maddoxes, they never boiled, but persistently gurgled, like the steady, monotonous wash of the sea against the shore; dangerous in their very persistency in any view they might have taken up.   But there was one very curious thing in all this which wrought very much to the *soi-disant* Richard Madingley's advantage. Influenced considerably by their enmity to Maurice Enderby, still further stimulated by the Reverend John Madingley declining to make their acquaintance, the two generals gradually worked themselves into the belief that John Madingley was an impostor.

It's astonishing how it is possible to persuade one's self to a belief in accordance with one's wishes, albeit we have no facts whatever to justify that opinion, and the Maddoxes and the Prauns were not at all people to keep what they thought to themselves. The consequence of all this was, that, far from suspicion falling upon the impostor, there was a lurking misgiving that the Reverend John Madingley was not what he represented himself to be; in the

eyes of the Prauns and the Maddoxes a
clergyman like Maurice Enderby, who
"dabbled in horse-racing," would be capable
of almost anything; they would hardly
have hesitated at almost openly insinuating
that the whole thing was a fraud but for
one fact; there was no getting over that:
General Shrewster knew and visited the
Reverend Mr. Madingley, and he was not
only above suspicion but carried far too
many guns to be assailed with impunity;
he might have been imposed upon, but it
was not likely, nor did even General Praun
feel that he should care about hinting *that*
to him. Shrewster's social position was
beyond dispute, and he had more than once
shown that he could say very bitter things
when provoked. Tunnleton had long ago
come to the conclusion that Shrewster was
a man to be let alone.

But a man who was made wonderfully

uneasy by all these varied rumours was Mr.
Molecombe. He was pledged to give his
daughter to this young man Richard Madingley. Here was his kinsman, from whom,
according to his own account, he expected to
inherit this Yorkshire property, and that
kinsman firmly but politely refused to see
Mr. Molecombe; although the banker had
written and explained the peculiar relations
under which he stood to Richard Madingley,
the recluse of Bingwell, although actually
residing in Tunnleton, kept his doors reso-
lutely closed upon him. Then these sinister
rumours reached his ears that the Rev. John
Madingley was an impostor, and this, with
the prolonged absence of his son-in-law that
was to be, still further increased the banker's
uneasiness. It was difficult for him to get
—not at the real state of things, but even at
what people thought; it was not likely that
men like Generals Praun and Maddox would

confide their suspicions to him, and a wholesome respect for General Shrewster made them
rather shy of expressing their opinion publicly.
The banker was much attached to his child,
and that he should feel uncomfortable about
her engagement was only natural, and there
could be no doubt about it, that just at present Mr. Richard Madingley's real *status*
was under suspicion. General Shrewster was
the only man behind the scenes, for John
Madingley had not even confided to the
Enderbys that he knew nothing whatever
of this young gentleman who had thought
proper to claim kinship with him. Shrewster
was, what he would have termed, watching
the match with great interest. "Madingley's
quite right," he would mutter to himself,
"in waiting for this impostor to show his
hand; unless he has heard of John Madingley's arrival, and got scared, he is bound
to make the first move, and then it will be a

case of checkmate almost immediately. The Scotland Yard people are right; we must allow this young gentleman a little more rope in order to make his discomfiture a certainty. However, if he should come back to Tunnleton there will be no doubt about that, and in any case it is clearly John Madingley's duty to interfere, and prevent Edith Molecombe being married to this man.

Mr. Pick's business being at length brought to a conclusion, it was settled that he should run down to Tunnleton that evening in the assumed character of Dick's uncle, and see what he thought of things. Madingley at once telegraphed to his servants to have dinner and a spare bed made ready, and a little before six he and Mr. Pick settled themselves comfortably in a first-class carriage and started for their destination.

There was only one other passenger, and
he was apparently absorbed in his cigar and
evening paper. Dick cast one long keen
glance at him, and then, coming to the conclusion that he had never seen the stranger
before, began conversing in a desultory way
about the past Ascot and Goodwood. Bob
Grafton, for he was the stranger, pricked up
his ears, as he always did when the talk ran
in that groove, but refrained from joining in
it. Suddenly he became haunted with the
idea that he had met the elder of his com-
panions before, and yet for the life of him
he could not recollect where or who he was.
The man was like a dim shadow of the
past connected in Grafton's mind with some
unpleasant incident. Ever and anon he
stole furtive glances over his paper at Mr.
Pick, but it was of no use ; the bookmaker was
to him like the blurred photograph of some

one he had known, but now failed to recognise.

On arrival at Tunnleton Bob got out, for
he was on his way to Bridge Court, and
purposed taking a fly from the station to
convey him thither. Rather to his astonishment his fellow-travellers followed his example, and as they drove off Grafton asked
the porter, who was busied with his luggage,
whether he knew them.

"The young un's Mr. Madingley, sir, but
I never saw the other gentleman before."

"Madingley!" exclaimed Grafton, as he
jumped into his fly. "I have it—that's the
fellow who found out John Madingley's mare
was lame at Epsom, and got such a lot of
money out of her for the Oaks—Pick, the
bookmaker, and if all that was said about
it was true, nobody was more likely to have
early information inasmuch as he was accused

of causing it. What can have brought that
precious scoundrel to Tunnleton ? "

"All right, Phillips; here we are," said
Dick Madingley, as his well-trained servant
opened the door the moment the fly stopped.
Take my uncle's things up to his room;
dinner in a quarter of an hour; and where
have you put my letters ? "

"You will find them on the mantel-piece
in the drawing-room, sir," and as he spoke
Dick fancied Mr. Phillips eyed Mr. Pick
with no little surprise and curiosity. But
apparently the man saw he was observed,
for he turned hastily away and disappeared
to attend to his duties.

"All fancy, I suppose," muttered Dick,
"there's nothing remarkable in my having
an uncle. Most people have till stricken in
years, and yet somehow that beggar Phillips
struck me as looking astonished. Now for
my letters: hum, small tradesmen's accounts,

a tea at the Torkeslys, will I join a house-dinner at the club, an invitation or two for garden-parties, and, hum! a note from my papa-in-law as is to be. 'Will I call as soon as I return? is most anxious to see me on a matter of great importance.' Now what maggot has he got in his head. However, I don't mean to see him to-night, to-morrow will do for him. Dinner and a bottle of wine's the first thing, anyway."

During dinner young Madingley kept up the farce and was extremely civil to his apochryphal uncle. Phillips's face gave no sign, though nothing escaped his keen eyes, and some of Mr. Pick's *gaucheries* might have put a less thoroughly trained servant off his balance; that gentleman, indeed, was not above harpooning anything he fancied with his own fork, and utterly ignored salt-spoons while his knife was in his hand,

plunging the blade in freely when wanting
that condiment. The meal over, and Mr.
Pick having pronounced it a very pretty
notion of a feed, the book-maker settled
down to a cigar and brandy and water.
Champagne he understood, but the best of
claret had no attractions for him.

" Look here, old man," said Dick, " you've
got all you want in the way of tobacco, &c.
and there's books of all sorts on those
shelves. I just want to slip down to the
club for an hour, and hear what's been going
on while I was away. Necessary, you see,
in the rather ticklish game I'm playing to
have the gossip of the place at my finger-
ends."

" Quite right. Don't you mind me. I've
a shrewd suspicion you're out of your depth
already. You can't keep too close an eye
on the current. Let it once turn against
you, and the sooner you slope the better."

" You're right.   Shall see you when I come back ; " and, with a nod to his friend, Dick took up his hat and sallied out into the night-air.

CHAPTER IX.

THE GAME ABOUT UP.

MR. PICK, left to his own reflections, began
in his parlance to reckon up the trumps in
their hand. "Yes, this sort of crib and
turn-out looks like money, and as for Dick's
name he's always gone under that of Madingley, and that he's no relation to old John
is no fault of his. He's quite willing to be-
long to the family *if* they'll let him. It was
a very good plant to come down here and look
out for a wife with money, and, according

to Dick, it looks like coming off if he can carry on a little longer. But there's one very awkward corner to get round. These swells always go in for what they call settlements—means, I suppose, putting down your picture cards and showing what money you've got and where you keep it. Now Dick must come to grief over that. He's only one chance, to run away with the girl and trust to the old man coming round afterwards. It's a risky game, and I shall charge pretty high for what I put into it."

Then Mr. Pick selected a novel from the book-case and sat down to enjoy for the twentieth time the account of the great "Oriel" trial in Digby Grand; for, like most men, Mr. Pick enjoyed the description of life and scenes within his own immediate experience. But he had not been reading long when the opening of the house-door announced the return of Dick Madingley.

"It's all U P," exclaimed that worthy; "and the sooner you clear out of Tunnleton the better."

"Why, what has happened?" inquired Mr. Pick.

"John Madingley is here, and has been for the last week. All Tunnleton knows it."

"Whew!" whistled Mr. Pick. "Yes, you're right—you are knocked out of time. Now the next thing is to get out as easy as we can."

"I don't know about *easy*," replied Dick. "I should think we had better get out as quick as we can."

"Now, look here, young man," replied Mr. Pick, impressively; "you can't be said to have my experience of tight places, and there's many an awkward circumstance in a man's career may be got over if he'll only just *brass it out*; now, I have no intention of putting myself in a bustle, I can tell you."

"Why, good gracious!" exclaimed Dick; "you come down here as John Madingley, and here's the very man himself in the town, what the deuce are you thinking of?"

"Never mind what I came down for; no one has heard you call me anything but 'uncle' as yet. Can't you have an uncle on your mother's side as well as your father's? Bless you, my boy, I'm your Uncle Popkins, or anything else you like to call me — bar Madingley — as for that 'uncle,' you must stick to it that they misunderstood you."

"But you don't suppose that will satisfy old Molecombe, do you?" replied Dick.

"No; nor that you will marry his daughter," retorted the book-maker.

"I don't know about that," replied Dick, doggedly. "If I am not mistaken, Edith is really fond of me, and when that is the case a girl don't throw you over just because her father says ' no.' "

" Ah ! then you *do* think that probable ? "

" Never had a doubt about it," rejoined Dick, sententiously ; " when it came to the settlements it was hardly likely that any hankey-pankey work you or I could manage would blind a man of business like Molecombe. No, I'll take your advice, and play the game out. I shall have to see Molecombe to-morrow, and no doubt get my dismissal when I disclaim all connexion with John Madingley."

" Good," said Mr. Pick, sententiously ; " it comes exactly to what I reckoned it up at when you were out. Run away with the girl, if you can, and trust to the stony-hearted father relenting afterwards. I don't mean putting much money into the business, I tell you, but I'll stay with you a week, and find you enough to carry on for a month on the old terms; if it don't come off in that time, you had better give it up. And now, my boy, I'm off to bed." And so saying, Mr. Pick lit his bedroom candle, and nodded good-night to his companion.

Dick Madingley sat lost in thought for some few minutes after the book-maker's departure. He possessed considerable experience of how far an off-hand manner, unlimited assurance, and the possession of ready money, will impose upon society. He was utterly unprincipled, and had for some time come to the conclusion that his first stepping-stone to fortune was to marry money. He liked Edith Molecombe, but, nice-looking girl though she was, he, nevertheless, was no whit in love with her. The question was, whether the speculation was good enough. The banker must have money, and, storm and rave though he might at the outset, yet when the thing was irrevocable he could not but forgive his only child. As for his past, Dick thought there would be not much trouble in burying that. It would be easy to ignore his present situation, and one or two of like character which he had previously held. Fool! as if the irrevocable past was not always dogging man's footsteps, and, obscure as his career may have been, rising up against him in the days of his splendour. It is no use; a man who knew you when you kept that grocery store in Islington confronts you sooner or later, when you soar to the glories of Cromwell Road.

However, this never crossed Dick's brain. He saw no further, and it was very possible to persuade Edith Molecombe to trust herself to him, and that, once married, her father's forgiveness would be a mere matter of time; and, with a firm determination to pursue his love-suit to the bitter end, Mr. Madingley followed his friend's example.

The next morning Dick, strongly advised by Mr. Pick, determined to take the bull by the horns, and, to use that worthy's expression, "have it out with his guv'nor-in-law" at once.

"Now, you know what you've got to say," said Mr. Pick. "Say it, say it strong, and then come the indignant dodge. Kicked out you'll be; that'll be the end of the first move. If the young woman means sticking to you, you'll know all about it before the week's out. Now then, off you go, and leave me to explore the beauties of Tumuleton."

Dick Madingley was blessed with plenty of nerve, and it was with the most unblushing effrontery that he knocked at the banker's door, and requested to see Mr. Molecombe.

He was informed that gentleman was out, upon which Dick expressed great annoyance, and, making his way to the drawing-room, told the servant to let Miss Molecombe know that he was waiting to see her. This request the man very naturally complied with, and, having shown Mr. Madingley into the empty drawing-room, went off at once in quest of his young mistress.

A very few minutes, and then the door opened and Edith Molecombe sprang forward to greet her lover.

"Oh, Dick!" she exclaimed, "what a long time you have been away from me."

"Soothing to my vanity to think you have found it so," he replied, "but I could not get away before; business arrangements consequent on our marriage detained me; and you know, dearest, how slow lawyers are about these sort of things. But, sit down, Edith, I want to have a little serious talk with you."

"Yes," replied the girl, as she seated herself on the sofa. "You haven't bad news to tell me, have you, Dick?"

"No, nothing very bad, though I must own I'm not a little annoyed, and, if you really care for me and will stick to me, I shan't so much mind."

"Why you know I will, Dick. Have not I promised?" she continued, almost in a whisper, "and do you think I'd go back from that promise?"

"No, I think I can trust you," he replied, "but during my absence a very awkward misunderstanding has arisen it seems. Mr. John Madingley—a well-known man up in Yorkshire—has taken up his abode in Tunnleton. Because his name happens to be the same as mine, and because I rather foolishly bragged of how good an uncle mine was to me, and what great expectations I had from him, I find all the people here have jumped to the conclusion that this Mr. John Madingley is that uncle."

"We certainly all thought you had said so, and I think papa has called twice on him. It seems he is a great invalid and sees nobody, with the exception of General Shrewster and the Enderbys."

Dick gave a slight start. "Odd!" he muttered. "Old Shrewster and that prig of a parson are the two people in Tunnleton I dislike most."

"Well, Edith," he continued aloud, "how the misunderstanding arose I don't know— I certainly never meant to say that Mr. John Madingley was my uncle. A very distant connection, no doubt he is, but the uncle to whom I owe everything is staying with me now, and rejoices in the more commonplace name of Dobson."

Edith Molecombe said nothing for two or three minutes. She felt quite certain that Dick had, upon more than one occasion, said positively that John Madingley of Bingwell, Yorkshire, was his uncle. She knew her lover was lying, but then he was her lover, so she deliberately shut her eyes to the truth, and determined to believe that she was mistaken.

"I don't see much to be disturbed about in all this. You will, of course, have to explain it to papa."

"Exactly what I had hoped to do this morning," he replied quickly! "I only heard of the rumour late last night, and came up this morning both to see you and to set your father right on this point."

"Papa may feel a little annoyed at having fallen into a mistake—most people are – but I don't know that it is one of very great consequence."

"Ah! Edith—Edith darling. Can't you see," exclaimed Dick with well simulated passion, "that your father gave you to me under the misapprehension that I was heir to a nice estate in Yorkshire? When he finds that I only expect to inherit a more moderate income, and that my uncle, though as dear an old fellow as ever stepped, can lay claim to no particular family, I am afraid he will revoke his consent. Can I depend on you, Edith, not to give me up then, but to stand firm, and wait till time shall soften his disappointment?"

"Yes," she replied in clear resolute tones, "I promised myself to you because I loved you—of course we can't marry without something to live upon; but you won't find me grumble if we are not quite so rich as was expected."

"Thanks, my own brave girl," he replied, as he bent down and kissed her, "now I feel I can trust implicitly in you, I have no fears for the result, although I shall doubtless have to go through a stern probation as best I may. And now I am sure you will agree with me that the sooner I see your father and put a stop to this absurd rumour generally, the better."

"Yes," said Miss Molecombe, "it will be best so. I don't think you do papa quite justice. He may feel a little disappointed, just at first, but he is not the man to go back from his word on such slight grounds as those."

"You have taken quite a load off my breast; and now I must be off;" and, after again embracing his *fiancée*, Dick Madingley took his departure.

"Not a bad morning's work," he mused, as he strolled leisurely back to Tunnleton, for the banker's house, be it remembered, stood a little way outside the town. "If

Edith only sticks to me, and I think she will, old Molecombe will have to give in at last. It wouldn't do to talk to her about running away just yet, but when I am presented with "the key of the street" I shall be able to harangue on domestic tyranny, and point out that there is a period when parental oppression justifies daughters taking their lives into their own hands. It won't take very long to arrive at that stage, either."

Could Dick have been present at a little conversation in John Madingley's rooms, he would have realised that his next interview with Mr. Molecombe would probably be his last.

" I think," said General Shrewster, " it's time now, Madingley, for you to interfere. I hear this precious namesake of yours returned last night, and you really are in common justice bound to let Molecombe know that he is no relation of yours."

" I'm not quite clear I'm called upon to interfere at all in the matter; Mr. Molecombe has thought proper to identify himself with the faction here that are apparently endeavouring to make Tunnleton impossible for Maurice and his wife to live in."

" I don't think that has anything to do with it," interrupted Maurice. I can't altogether blame Mr. Molecombe because he has thought fit to credit malicious charges brought against me; but surely, sir, it is your duty to unmask this young scoundrel, and save Miss Molecombe from such a terrible fate as her marriage with him would be."

" You go a little too fast," replied John Madingley, quietly. " Just bear in mind, that, whatever we may think, all we know positively is that he is no nephew of mine."

" Perfectly true," remarked Shrewster, " but I agree with Enderby, that it is only right you should let Molecombe know that fact at once."

Thus urged, John Madingley sat down and wrote a brief note to the banker, in which he said, "that, it having come to his ears that a certain Mr. Richard Madingley, whom he understood was engaged to be married to Miss Molecombe, had stated that he was nephew and heir to him (John Madingley), he begged to inform Mr. Molecombe that the gentleman in question was no relation, and that he had never heard of his existence until he himself arrived in Tunnleton some three weeks ago."

"There," he said, "I think that meets the case, anyhow it is all I virtually know of the matter, and Mr. Molecombe must do as he thinks best on that knowledge."

"Oh! that will be quite sufficient," cried Maurice. "No father could dream of giving his daughter to a man capable of uttering such a gross falsehood as that."

"I hope you're right, Mr. Enderby," said General Shrewster, "but, mark my words, he is a precious cunning, plausible, young gentleman, and I should not be the least surprised if he carried off Miss Molecombe after all. If he is the arrant adventurer I suspect him to be, Edith Molecombe's money is her great attraction in his eyes. And the tenacity with which men of this class cling to a purpose of this sort is marvellous," and then the general took up his hat and departed.

CHAPTER X.

FAMILY JARS.

ALTHOUGH Dick Madingley had failed to
see Mr. Molecombe he was not left long
in ignorance of that gentleman's decision ;
indeed, in the course of the day he received
two notes from the banker ; the first merely
requested him to call the next morning on
a matter of considerable importance, the
second informed him that there would be
no necessity to do so : that he, Mr. Molecombe, had received a communication from

the Reverend John Madingley not only entirely repudiating him as a nephew, but disowning any relationship with him whatever. "As," continued the banker, "you have persistently and distinctly always referred me to your uncle, I need scarcely say that my whole belief in your account of yourself is shaken, and you cannot be surprised at my refusing to consent to any engagement between my daughter and a man about whose antecedents I know nothing, further than that he has represented himself to me as the acknowledged heir of a gentleman who had never even heard of him until about a fortnight ago. You will therefore understand that your engagement to my daughter is at an end, as also is our acquaintance," and then the banker wound up formally with, he had "the honour to be, &c."

But Dick Madingley was not going to

take his dismissal quietly.   He replied to
Mr. Molecombe's letter, and repeated the
same specious story of a misunderstanding
that he had detailed to Edith, pointed out
that the uncle from whom he really had
expectations, and to whom he owed everything, was now staying with him, and that
if Mr. Molecombe would only consent to be
introduced to Mr. Dobson he would see how
the mistake arose.

But the banker's reply was very short
and uncompromising; he briefly pointed out
that Richard Madingley had several times
deliberately stated that John Madingley
was his uncle, a fact which that gentleman
emphatically denied.   He could not refuse to
believe the latter on this point, and therefore
had no alternative but to regard Mr. Richard
Madingley as having wilfully misrepresented
his social position, and therefore begged to
decline any further intercourse with him.

"Kicked out," said Dick meditatively, as he handed the letter to his Mentor; "well, I expected that."

"Just so," replied Mr. Pick; "well, if old Molecombe won't let you in at the front door there's nothing for it but the young lady should steal out at the back. Yes, Master Dick, if you press the siege hard enough you ought to persuade her to make a bolt of it before a fortnight is out. However, I shan't be able to give you much more of my society; I have had my holiday and must be off to York races on Monday."

It was evident to the precious pair that Mr. Pick could be of no further assistance in the prosecution of this sordid love-suit; that was for Dick to pursue alone. As has been before said, he was of a bitter and vindictive nature, and he felt that it would afford him much satisfaction to laugh at the banker's beard by carrying off his daughter

in the face of the curt dismissal he had
received, and the fates were fighting for
him in a way which, though common-place,
would not have happened in the case of a
more judicious man than Mr. Molecombe.
It was a sore blow to the banker's pride to
think that all Tunnleton would be talking
of his daughter's engagement with one
whom he felt little doubt now was a mere
specious adventurer, and he was foolish
enough to visit his annoyance upon Edith.
He delighted in painting Dick Madingley's
conduct in the blackest terms. His daughter
stood up for her lover with much spirit; she
had determined to believe Dick's own
version of the story, and shut her eyes to
what she knew to be the real state of the
case. She was very much in love, and what
girl under those circumstances would not
stand up for her lover, let his wrong-doing
be what it might ? ''

There was much stormy converse with the
twain upon this point, with the usual result,
that Edith believed more strongly in her
lover than ever.

To open a clandestine correspondence
with Miss Molecombe was easy work for
Dick, who was personally acquainted with
all the dependants of the establishment, and
the female servant who would not assist in
the promotion of a love affair, more especially when liberally handselled, is rarely
met with. Dick's passionate notes quickly
found their way to their destination, and
that they contained entreaties for a rendez-
vous need scarcely be mentioned. There
were plenty of secluded walks around Tuunle-
ton, and in these long summer afternoons
there was no one to know of Edith Molecombe's coming and going. The awkward
disappointment gave her an excuse for
rather holding aloof from Tunnleton society

for the present, and so day after day she wandered through the fields and woods with her
scapegrace lover. The strong common sense
that she naturally possessed would whisper
to her now and then that Dick's love-tale
was hardly veracious, but the glamour of her
passion closed her eyes, and if she could not
quite believe that it was all misunderstanding, and that he had never represented himself as the nephew of John Madingley, yet she
deemed the falsehood had been perpetrated
because of the great love Dick bore her.

" Even supposing," he would argue, " that
I had said so, which I deny, when a fellow
cares about a girl, and is just wild to call her
his own, it's no great crime if he a little
bounces about his position to her relations
in order to carry his point. A man who
is a man don't stick at trifles when he's over
head and ears in love with a girl, and I don't
think, Edith, I should stand at much to win

you," and Miss Molecombe in her infatuation thought Richard Madingley one of the most chivalrous of men, and failed to discern the utter selfishness of his character. "Your father," continued Dick, "is behaving like a parent of the last century; he has no business to treat you in the way he is doing, it is shameful that he should play the tyrant in this bygone fashion; remember you are of age, and no parent can dictate to you on a matter of this kind."

"Oh! Dick," she cried; "I am always standing up for you; I have told papa again and again that I will not sit by and hear you abused, and I intend to stand to my promise, and will marry nobody but you."

"You are a dear, good girl," he replied, "and if your father cannot be brought to listen to reason we shall have to take the law into our own hands. I want you for yourself, darling, and not merely because

your father can make you a handsome allow-
ance if he chooses."

" I don't quite understand you, Dick, but
I couldn't marry you without papa's consent,
I couldn't indeed ! I will be true to you,
but we must wait, he will come round in
time."

"By all means," rejoined Dick, "give him
time, though it is hardly fair to expect us to
waste our lives because he happened to mis-
understand what I said—but never mind,
darling, I know you're true as steel, and as
long as that is the case I will bear this
injustice as best I may."

It was ingeniously put ; Dick Madingley
was posing before his *fiancée* as the victim
of cruel injustice. He drew her closer to
him, and as they strolled leisurely down a
briar-scented lane a more loverlike couple
could scarcely have been seen ; and this was
precisely the view that a tall muscular

young man, who had just reached a stile leading into the lane some thirty or forty yards behind them, took of affairs.

Maurice Enderby, for it was he, paused ere he mounted the stile. He recognised the couple before him at a glance, and had no wish to intrude upon them, but he felt sorely puzzled as to what he ought to do under the circumstances. He knew, as did all Tumuleton, by this time, that Mr. Molecombe had withdrawn his consent to Edith's marriage; he believed, as did many other people, that Richard Madingley was an impostor; still it was perfectly clear that Miss Molecombe had not given him up and did not share that opinion. Maurice Enderby sat for some time on that stile thinking what he should do. It did not require much knowledge of the world to know how clandestine meetings with an unprincipled scamp like Dick Madingley would terminate.

He could not bear the idea of any girl becoming the prey of a reckless adventurer
such as Dick. He could not stand still
and see Edith Molecombe, in a moment of
madness, consign herself to life-long misery.
But how was he to interfere? It was a
very delicate matter to touch upon. He
might communicate his discovery to Mr.
Molecombe, and throw that gentleman into
a perfect tempest of indignation, but it
struck Maurice that would be more likely
to precipitate an elopement than avert it.
In vain did Maurice cudgel his brains; he
could think of no other means of interfering
except through the medium of Edith's father,
and he felt instinctively that would produce more harm than good. In the mean-
time the lovers had got well out of sight,
and he could now pursue his way home.
Maurice felt that he should very much
like to take counsel with somebody as to
what he had best do—but with whom? Most

decidedly he did not wish his discovery bla-
zoned abroad. Should he confide the matter
to General Shrewster, and take his advice on
the subject? He was a clear-headed man and
not given to babble; however, he was not
destined to require the general's services upon
this occasion; for, to his great delight, on
arriving at his own house, he found Bob
Grafton chatting merrily over the tea-table
with Mrs. Enderby, and it flashed across
him that a thorough man of the world like
Grafton was just the very man to take into
his confidence.

Grafton was in high spirits; news and
gossip of every kind fell from his lips. He
touched on pretty well everything that was
talked about—musically, politically, socially,
and wound up by congratulating Mrs. Enderby with mock gravity upon her successful *début* as an owner of race-horses.
Bessie's face became serious directly.

"Don't jest about that, please, Mr. Grafton. There is no denying we have been very fortunate, and that the money has been a great boon to us; but I can't help feeling that it is an ill-omened present, as we shall discover in the end."

"Nonsense, Mrs. Enderby! There can be no harm in what you do; indeed, as a matter of fact you don't win it; you've the luck to possess a jolly old uncle who gives you half *his* winnings, which he can well afford to do. I only wish I had an uncle so charged with right feeling. And now I must say good-bye; it's a good stretch back to Bridge Court."

"I'll walk part of the way with you, Bob," said Maurice, as he took up his hat, and the pair descended the stairs together. "I want your advice on a rather ticklish point," he continued, when they found themselves outside the door. And then Maurice

told the whole story of Dick Madingley's
arrival in Tunnleton, how he had proclaimed
himself nephew and heir of John Madingley,
had become engaged to a young lady of the
place, and how that when John Madingley
himself appeared on the scene he had utterly
repudiated all knowledge of his namesake.

Grafton listened with great attention and
no little amusement. " What a precious
young scamp!" he exclaimed, as Maurice
finished, "and by Jove! what a sell for him
John Madingley turning up at the finish!
However, of course that burst him up, and
his matrimonial speculation is all over now."

" That is just what it isn't," rejoined Maurice. "Molecombe broke off his daughter's
engagement, and turned this young gentleman out of the house with the utmost
promptitude. But the fellow still lingers in
the place, as I happened to discover to-day,
and is still making clandestine love to Miss

Molecombe. Now this is what I want to consult you about. I don't wish to meddle, I don't desire to make a scandal. If I inform her father——"

" Oh, nonsense!" interrupted Bob, energetically; " from your description of him, he would lock her up, and then she would be off before twenty-four hours were over her head. No, there's only one way out of a thing like this. We must deal with Dick Madingley. We must either bounce him out of Tunnleton, or buy him, but I think we can manage to do the former. You must know that when I came down the beginning of the week my attention was attracted by one of my two fellow-travellers. The man's face haunted me. I knew I had seen it before, and under unpleasant circumstances. Rather to my surprise, they both got out at Tunnleton, and the porter told me that the younger man of the two was

Mr. Richard Madingley. The name brought it all back to me. I recollected my man then. It was a Mr Pick, a leg who was strongly suspected of being actively engaged in the laming of a horse of John Madingley's at Epsom. Like most of these cases, it couldn't be proved, but of one thing there was no doubt, that nobody benefited by that mare's accident so largely as Mr. Pick, and from the heavy amount he had betted against her it seemed as if he had foreseen the accident that befell her at the eleventh hour."

" Still, although that is very corroborative of the opinion I have formed of Dick Madingley, I don't see how that is going to help us."

" It's not at all a bad card, my dear Maurice, in the game of bounce that we are about to play; that this young gentleman should be entertaining such a known scoundrel as Pick speaks volumes against him;

besides, didn't you tell me that he swaggered
a good deal about an uncle who is staying
with him whom he asserted to be the uncle
who owned the gold-mine, or whatever he
chose to call it.   Now I take it half Tunnleton could tell you who has been staying
with Mr. Richard Madingley this week, and
if it turns out, as I think it quite likely it
may do, that this thief Pick, the book-maker,
has been posing as that wealthy relative,
then my boy we've got the ace of trumps in
our hand, and now good-bye.   I'll be with
you to lunch to-morrow, and we'll snuff our
young friend out as soon as we have made
the necessary inquiries.

CHAPTER XI.

NOTICE TO QUIT.

THE morrow was rather an eventful day
with Maurice Enderby. In the first place
John Madingley took his departure; he was
extremely cordial in his farewell both to
Bessie and her husband. "I'll give you
what help I can, my lad," he said as he
bade Maurice good-bye, "in whatever you
turn your hand to; but you're no more fit
to be a parson than I was, though when they
come to tot up my ledger they'll find I've

been a good deal better clergyman than
they give me credit for; but remember,
things were very different when I began,
and what was thought no harm in a parson
doing in my younger days is looked upon
in quite another light now. You're in the
wrong groove, my boy; take an old man's
advice, think very seriously before you are
ordained priest, and remember if you want
a little money to start in another line I dare
say I can manage to find it for you." A
warm kiss to Bessie, a hearty wrench of the
hand to Maurice Enderby, and old John
Madingley was speeding once more towards
his northern home.

"I hope you've a decent lunch for Grafton," said Maurice to his wife, as they
strolled home from the station.

"Don't throw doubts upon my house-
keeping," replied Bessie, laughing, "the
fatted calf has been killed for Mr. Grafton,

and I don't think you'll have anything to complain of."

Bob Grafton turned up in due course, and did due justice to Mrs. Enderby's preparations; but no sooner was their meal disposed of, and they were left by Bessie to their own devices, than he at once plunged into the midst of things.

" I've asked a question here and there about Tunnleton this morning, and gathered a fact or two that will be useful to us. Only one person has stayed with Richard Madingley since he established himself here, that was his uncle, Mr. Dobson, who left again some two or three mornings ago. I've no earthly doubt that Mr. Pick and Mr. Dobson are identical, though what object Mr. Pick had in posing as this young man's uncle I don't know. I can imagine a score of good reasons for his changing his name. He may be veritably his uncle for all I know, but we've this fact to go upon, his relative is well known as a thoroughly unscrupulous book-maker, and is masquerading down here under an assumed name. The conclusion is obvious; he is known to have given utterance to a most mendacious statement regarding his kinship to John Madingley. You have fair grounds, therefore, for supposing that he is also down here under false colours. And now comes the question of how are we to put the screw on. What I propose is this, that you and I walk down to see him, tell him briefly, but sternly, that we give him forty-eight hours to clear out of Tumbleton, and that if he has not disappeared in that time you will feel it your duty to lay the facts that have come to your knowledge before the committee of the club."

"And suppose," replied Maurice, "he simply laughs at us, and tells us to do our worst?"

"Then hold your tongue and let me talk to him. You see, if what we know really *was* put before a committee of the club, they would feel bound to make him substantiate his social position. What scoundrels he may choose to know is no business of theirs, but doubts having arisen they have a right to insist upon his vindicating himself and show them that he is a gentleman and not a mere adventurer who has crept into their midst under false colours."

"And you think it possible, Bob, to keep Miss Molecombe's name out of the business altogether?"

"No, honestly, I don't; we will do our best; but an unprincipled blackguard like that is pretty certain to introduce it, even if he gives in and we carry our point; he is sure to spit all the venom he can; and look here, Maurice, you used to be able to hit terribly hard with the gloves when you were a freshman, and probably will be sorely tempted to knock Mr. Richard Madingley down before our interview is over. Mind, you must keep your temper. And now, the sooner we tackle this gentleman in his own den the better."

Mr. Richard Madingley, having made an excellent luncheon, was ruminating how things stood with him in Tunnleton. He was quite conscious that they were beginning to look askew at him at the club. They had no doubt there about his having represented himself to be John Madingley's nephew, and they were equally aware from General Shrewster that John Madingley had most clearly denied all relationship during his brief visit to Tunnleton. People who had opened their houses freely to Dick Madingley began now to repent their precipitation. Some few crusty old members, who had not benefited by Dick's hospitality.

were already whispering that "the fellow ought never to have been let in here, the committee are not half particular enough in their scrutiny." Let people once conceive a suspicion that you have deceived them, and that you are not what you represented yourself to be, and it is wonderful how willing they are to go into the other extreme, and believe any wild story to your detriment.

Dick felt that opinion was against him in Tunnleton. He could not but notice that many of his fair acquaintances, who had previously quite courted a bow from him, now seemed a little anxious to avoid meeting him, and when they did the old smiling salute degenerated into a frigid bend.

"Yes," he mused, "the game's about up here; well, it has served my turn very well, and I don't know that even the finish of it is not another trick in my favour! The

question of settlements would have been a
rock I must have split upon ; my only
chance would have been to run away with
Edith, and old Molecombe's angry breaking-
off of our engagement only makes it easier
to win her consent to that step. A few
days more, and I've no doubt I shall get
her to agree to it." But here Dick Madingley's reflections were somewhat rudely interrupted by an intimation from Phillips
that Mr. Enderby wished to see him.

" Mr. Enderby ! " exclaimed Dick in
great astonishment.

" Yes, sir," replied Phillips ; " he and
another gentleman, I don't know his name,
but he's often about Tunnleton, I believe ;
stops a good deal at Bridge Court, sir."

" Show them up to the drawing-room,
Phillips, and say I'll be with them in two
or three minutes. Enderby," he muttered,
" now what can he want with me ? I hate

him, and don't suppose he has much liking
for me. What can he have got to say to
me? As for the story about John Madingley, why all the town knows it by this time,
he can't have come with that precious discovery to me. And I don't think," said
Dick, meditatively, "he can possibly have
found out anything else; however, here
goes."

When Dick entered the drawing-room,
Maurice Enderby saluted him with a formal
bow, introduced the stranger who accom-
panied him as his friend Mr. Grafton, and
then, without further preface, he continued,

"I need scarcely say, Mr. Madingley,
that nothing but a matter of urgent importance would have justified this intrusion,
but if you will only listen to me patiently
for a few minutes I will endeavour to be
as brief as possible over a most unpleasant
business," and then, in pithy logical se-

quence, Maurice stated the facts with which we are already acquainted, and concluded by saying that all these things threw such grave doubts on the minds of both himself and his friend that he had no alternative but to make them public.

"And do you suppose, Mr. Enderby, that I feel called upon to inform you of all the details of my family history, of where I usually live, who are my intimate acquaintances, &c."

"No," replied Maurice, "that will be for the information of the club committee, and, as for family details, I can only trust that you will be rather more fortunate as regards uncles than you have been so far."

The shot told. A savage scowl passed across Dick Madingley's face, and he muttered something, of which "meddlesome parsons" was all that was audible. Bob Grafton, who had watched him keenly from the beginning of Maurice's statement, had noted, coolly though Dick took it, his slight start at the mention of Mr. Pick; he also noted the slightly nervous twitch with which he heard the threat of placing his case before the club committee. "That fellow will shut up when the pinch comes," thought Grafton.

"I have very little doubt, Mr. Enderby," rejoined Dick, with a sneer, "you are intimately acquainted with the members of the betting ring. It is not often that any gentleman manifests your interest in turf matters who is not in the habit of doing business with that fraternity. I am not aware that you ever saw my Uncle Dobson, but, even if you did, an accidental likeness to an unknown betting man hardly warrants the assertion that he is a supposititious relation"

Maurice hesitated for a moment, but

Grafton now cut into the conversation in quiet resolute fashion that somewhat awed Dick Madingley.

"Oh, no!" he said, "we don't make mistakes of that kind. I'm a racing man myself, and have known Mr. Pick by sight ever since he nobbled Marietta for the Oaks seven years ago. I travelled down from London in the same carriage with you and him ten days ago, and know perfectly well he passed in Tunnleton as your Uncle Dobson. Never had anybody else staying with you, you know, since you've been in Tunnleton. Can't be any mistake about it, you see."

"And what the devil have you got to do with it, I should like to know?" demanded Dick fiercely. "By what right do you interfere?"

"Right!" exclaimed Grafton, with a short laugh. "By the right that men put welshers out of the inclosure of the race-course, by the right that all men have to defend their brethren from fraud, by the acknowledged right and duty of every man to expose a swindler!"

"And you dare say this to me!" cried Dick, with a voice hoarse with passion.

"Yes," chimed in Maurice, "we not only say it, but, as Grafton says, it's our duty to say it. For the sake of some of those who have weakly trusted you, who have weakly welcomed you to their homes, and to whom this exposure must be a source of bitter shame, we are willing to hush it up as far as may be. Give us your word to leave Tunnleton within eight-and-forty hours, and we will stay our hands for that time; but after that remember everything we know is laid before the club committee, and your exposure is imminent."

"You may do as you like about that,"

rejoined Madingley, "I am quite willing to court investigation, and shall bring an action for libel against the pair of you to boot."

" No you won't," chimed in Grafton, "we are not going to be frightened by brag, and you don't mean fighting. You'll be out of Tunnleton in forty-eight hours."

" Do you know, sir," rejoined Dick, with inimitable assurance, " that I am engaged to be married to Miss Molecombe, and that——

" Her father kicked you out of the house a few days ago. Yes, we know all about that, and it is to avoid such annoyances as this that we suggest that you should leave Tunnleton quietly and at once—but leave Tunnleton you will, or find yourself cut by the whole community."

For a few minutes Dick reflected in dogged silence, then he said—

" Remember, I in no wise acknowledge that the allegations you make against me are true, although perhaps there is just that suspicion of truth in them that makes them difficult to disprove; but, gentlemen, my feelings are deeply involved as regards Miss Molecombe, and I utterly decline to leave Tunnleton for another week."

"Ha! in order that you may continue your clandestine meetings with that foolish girl," interposed Maurice hotly. "No, Mr. Madingley; forty-eight hours is the outside we give you, and I honestly believe that is twenty-four too long."

Dick looked at him for a moment.

"I suppose," he said, with an evil sneer, "that in the interests of morality you consider it necessary to keep strict espionage over your flock. I have heard of such shepherds, but never saw one of the dirty creatures before. You have been doing me the honour, I presume, of dogging my footsteps lately."

For an instant Maurice's fist clenched, his eyes flashed, the veins in his forehead stood out, and it was the veriest toss-up whether Dick Madingley measured his length on the carpet or not ; but a " steady, old man," from Grafton turned the scale, and with a mighty effort Maurice mastered his temper.

" I happened to see you walking with Miss Molecombe yesterday, and knowing, as indeed all Tumnleton knows, that her father had forbidden all intercourse between you, I don't scruple to say that such conduct on your part will make gossip all too busy with her name."

" Never mind going into all that," broke in Grafton, " it is quite beside the point. Mr. Madingley thoroughly understands us— we give him forty-eight hours to leave the place quietly. After that, we do our best to unmask an adventurer. No ; you needn't talk about libel—we'll chance that. Come along, Maurice, I don't think we need detain Mr. Madingley any longer; he quite understands us."

"I shall take my own course," blustered Dick.

"Just so," rejoined Grafton; "which will be a ticket to London by an early train to-morrow. Good-morning"

Dick Madingley vouchsafed not the slightest notice of their salutation, and, when the pair were outside the house, Maurice exclaimed—

"Thank heaven we are through with that. I never was so sorely tempted to inflict personal chastisement as I was a few minutes ago."

"No, I know, old man; but it would have weakened our game terribly, and a summons for assault is always an awkward thing for one of your profession. He's going right enough, never fear; but you were right in

one thing: we ought not to have given him
more than twenty-four hours; he's a vindictive, mischievous cur, that, and, mark me,
Maurice, if by any fluke he ever has a
chance of squaring accounts with you he
will do it; but he's a plausible beggar, and
there's no saying what he mayn't persuade
Miss Molecombe to do in the time we've
given him; however, we may console ourselves with one thing: if a young woman
in these days is bent upon marrying the
wrong man she will do it sooner or later
in spite of everybody. I turn off here, so
must say good-bye. I leave Bridge Court
in two or three days now, and if you happen
to want me *in re* Madingley you know my
London address."

Maurice Enderby walked home musing
over his interview with Dick Madingley.
He had done the best he could think of to
prevent Edith Molecombe falling into the

hands of the audacious adventurer who had ensnared her affections, but he was forced to admit that Grafton was right, and that, let the girl's father and friends do what they would, it must depend very much upon whether Edith could be brought to see the utter worthlessness of her lover. On one point of the interview Maurice looked back regretfully, and a faint smile played round his mouth as he muttered,

"No, I don't think I am suited to the profession. Ah, if I hadn't been a parson how I would have knocked that fellow down!"

CHAPTER XII.

HER HEART FAILED HER.

DICK MADINGLEY paced the drawing-room
for a good half-hour after his visitors left
him. He had decided before their coming
that it behoved him to quit Tunnleton very
shortly, and, except for Edith Molecombe,
it would suit him just as well to leave the
day after to-morrow as a week or two later;
he would not see Edith this afternoon, as
he was well aware that she had an engagement that would prevent her meeting him,

and further, she had told him that she must in-
evitably be discovered if their meetings were
too frequent. She was to see him to-morrow,
and the question was, should he be able to persuade her to elope with him on the following
day ? Dick had a pretty genius for intrigue;
no, he would not go by the morning train, for
that was the train which Tunnleton chiefly
affected, for the obvious reason that it gave
them a long day in town ; no, he would go
by the mid-day train, and, if he could persuade Edith to come with him, well, he
would take her ; they must not go together,
and he thought if Edith travelled up second-
class and closely veiled she would run little
risk of recognition ; he would get her ticket
for her and contrive to slip it into her hand
as she passed into the station; once there
she must stick closely to the ladies' room
till the train came in, and then, if she
slipped quickly into her carriage, he thought

in the confusion she would escape all observation. Would he be able to persuade
her to this step so abruptly? Dick Madingley had great confidence in his power over
the girl; if that confounded parson had
only given him another week or ten days
he would have had no fears as to the result,
but most girls are startled at the idea when
such a step is first proposed to them. Dick
knew this, and, though by no means troubled
with diffidence, felt that he might not
succeed.

Grafton read him truly; he might bluster
about what he was going to do, but Dick
Madingley knew a good deal better than
to risk an inquiry into his social status by
any of the Tunnleton people. No, he would
settle the few bills he owed in the town
that afternoon, for Dick was not an adventurer of the petty sort that swindles the
trades-people of the place in which they

conduct their campaign; he flew at higher game than that, and, but for the inopportune appearance of John Madingley on the scene, would probably have won the prize for which he strove. This aim, just now, was a wealthy marriage, and in Edith Molecombe he imagined he had found a young lady who must eventually come into a good bit of money, and whose father, if he liked, could behave very handsomely to her at present. He might have had to run away with her in any case, but he would have figured in a very different light before Tunnleton had his imposition regarding John Madingley not been discovered. Yes, if ever a man of his temperament had a debt to settle with another he had with Maurice Enderby, and he vowed that, should the chance ever come, Mr. Enderby should be paid in full. Curiously enough his animosity was but slightly roused as regarded

Grafton, but his antipathy to Maurice was of long standing and had increased in intensity day by day: this was the culmination of it, and Dick Madingley was not likely to be very scrupulous should he ever see his way to revenge.

Dick Madingley had been sitting on the stile leading into Kilroe Wood a good half-hour, and was beginning to wonder whether Edith would keep her appointment, when a light step behind him caught his ear, and, in another moment, Miss Molecombe was by his side.

"I am very sorry I am late, Dick, but I had a good deal of difficulty to get here at all. I can't help thinking they suspect something; papa said last night that he could not think what you were still hanging about Tunnleton for, a place in which, he said, you were utterly discredited, and further added that if he for one moment thought it were on my account he would pack me off to my aunt in Wales, and then, as usual, we came to high words, which ended in my flouncing out of the room and having a good cry upstairs."

" It is as I thought, darling," replied Mr. Madingley, " your father is commencing to play the domestic tyrant. As long as you stand to me, you will be continually talked at. It is too much to ask of any girl to bear that. Better tell your father at once, dear, that you give me up, and then they would let you alone."

" You don't mean it, Dick, you can't; you know I wouldn't give you up."

" I think perhaps it would be best for you, dearest. I must leave this to-morrow, and though, as long as there is a hope of winning your hand I shall be true, yet it is trying you too hard to hold you to your engagement. Tell your father it is broken."

" Dick ! Dick don't think so meanly of me; do you think I cannot wait and suffer patiently for your sake ?" and Edith thought how unselfish and chivalrous her lover was in endeavouring to make their parting as easy as possible for her.

" Yes, it must be so," replied Madingley. " It will be sad and dreary work for me, but there is no alternative, unless —— " and here he paused abruptly, with apparent confusion.

" Unless what ? " she exclaimed, anxiously.

" Nothing, nothing. Don't ask me : I never ought to have said what I did ; forget those last two or three words."

" No, I claim to hear what you were about to suggest," replied Edith, " if there is any other course open to us, I've a right to decide whether I will take it."

At first Dick Madingley positively refused to explain himself, but gradually the specious impostor allowed Edith to draw from him that she might be freed from all annoyances and their mutual happiness secured if she could make up her mind to run away with him the next morning.

At first Edith was frightened out of her life at the bare suggestion, but gradually as Dick unfolded his scheme, and pointed out to her the extreme simplicity of it, she began to listen to him, and before they parted she had pledged herself to meet him at the Tunnleton Station, and elope with him by the midday train, and then Miss Molecombe scampered home with a heightened pulse and a heart beating with unnatural rapidity.

If Edith wanted any strengthing in her resolution it was administered to her that night. Business at the bank had gone a little awry; it was not that anything serious had occurred, but an unpleasant mistake had been made with regard to one of their best customers' accounts, and the customer in

question, who was a wealthy and irascible
man, had gone the length of blowing up Mr.
Molecombe in his own bank parlour about the
carelessness of his subordinates. That Mr.
Molecombe had passed that on, and made
things pretty lively all round for the subordinates in question, it is almost needless to
add, but unluckily he had not wholly worked
off his irritation at his place of business,
and poured forth the remnant of his wrath
on his own family. Having pronounced the
cook utterly incompetent, and marvelled why
Mrs. Molecombe continued to keep a woman
so incapable of cooking a mutton chop, having informed his butler that he was an idiot,
who, after many years' experience, seemed to
know less about what should be the proper
temperature of the wine than a charity
school-boy, he, when the servants withdrew,
commenced to talk *at* his daughter, perhaps
the most exasperating form of attack: he

said nothing to Edith, and poured forth a flood of ridicule and abuse to his wife on the subject of Dick Madingley. At last Edith, springing to her feet, exclaimed, with flashing and tear-stained eyes, that she would bear it no longer, that she believed none of these lies that were circulated about Mr. Madingley, and that even if they were true he might recollect that with his own consent Dick Madingley had been affianced to her for weeks. That she had given him her love, and, come what might, she would not sit still and hear him thrown stones at. "I can bear these taunts no longer, and sooner than continue to endure them I shall seek a home elsewhere."

"You had better seek your pillow at once, Miss," replied Mr. Molecombe, furiously, "and as for the home, if this is not good enough for you, I'll make arrangements for you to reside with your aunt in Wales.

The scenery is magnificent, and as for society I believe there are the goats," concluded Mr. Molecombe with grim irony.

"Good-night, mamma," said Edith in a low tone, and without ever glancing at her father she quickly left the room.

Mrs. Molecombe was a rather weak woman and stood in no little awe of her domineering husband, but she loved her daughter dearly, and no sooner had the door closed than she took up the cudgels on her behalf.

"You are too hard upon her, Alick, you are indeed," she exclaimed, "the girl has met with a bitter disappointment and is naturally very sore at heart. Why cannot you give the wound time to heal? Why will you not suffer her to do her best to forget him? You don't know the suffering you inflict. You don't know that when a girl has given her heart away what a desert life seems to her when she is told that her lover is worthless and that she must give him up.

"Confound it, woman," rejoined Mr. Molecombe, in milder tones and with no little contrition for his past ill-temper, "you don't mean to say that it was my fault we did not discover this Madingley was a liar and a scoundrel sooner."

"No, Alick; but cannot you understand that alluding to her lover's iniquities is dropping nitric acid into Edith's wounds. Pray, pray, leave the subject alone before her. Don't let the name of Richard Madingley ever pass your lips."

"Well, well, perhaps I'm wrong, but the whole thing, you know, has been so deuced disagreeable. I am quite the laughing-stock of the town, and then Edith makes me mad by standing up for the young villain; but I'll do my best, I'll try not to say any thing

about him before Edith, and if, as I hope,
he clears out of Tunnleton before many days
are over, that will make it all the easier."

The banker lingered over his breakfast
the next morning in the hope of making
friends with his daughter, but Edith's maid
reported that her mistress was suffering from
a bad headache, and wanted nothing but a
cup of tea in her own room. Mr. Molecombe
of course went up to see her, but Edith declared she was suffering chiefly from the
effects of a bad night and only wanted quiet
and to be let alone.   She had made up her
mind that this would be her best chance
of escaping all observation; it was easy
enough to get out of the house and make her
way to the station, but the difficulty was to
carry a hand-bag with her; more baggage
she dared not attempt, but even that little
would attract attention, should any of the
servants catch sight of her departure.   Once

clear of the house, and the getting to the station by roads by which she was not likely to meet acquaintances was easy. In due course she rang for her maid and dressed, then ordered a cup of strong beef-tea and desired not to be disturbed till luncheon time. A quarter of an hour afterwards, and, closely veiled, hot though the weather was, with her dressing-bag in her hand, she stole down the back stairs into the garden; a light shawl thrown carelessly over her arm veiled the dressing-bag. One piece of lawn dangerously open to observation was safely crossed, and then Edith plunged into the shrubberies and felt safe. No chance of meeting any one now, unless it was some under-gardener. No. She felt the perils of her enterprise were over until she arrived in the purlieus of Tunnleton Station.

Edith passed into the booking-office unnoticed, and then stood irresolute, not know-

ing how to act. She glanced at the clock,
and saw there was a quarter of an hour yet
before the train was due. Had she better
take her ticket while the office was as yet
uncrowded, or leave the obtaining of it to
Dick ?

While she still hesitated a voice whispered
in her ear—

"Go into the waiting-room at once;
don't come out till the bell rings, and then
jump as quickly as possible into the nearest
carriage," while at the same time she felt
her ticket slipped into her hand.

Without turning her head she made her
way into the waiting-room as directed, and
there, in a state of some trepidation, awaited
the signal of the coming train. A few
minutes and the bell rang out its warning
for passengers to take their seats. Grasping
her dressing-bag, Edith made her way
swiftly to the platform; but as she crossed

the threshold stopped paralysed, for there, not half a score paces from her, stood her father in animated conversation with some gentleman, whom he was apparently seeing off to London. To reach her part of the train she must pass close to him, and she could hardly hope that he would not instantly recognise her. Her heart failed her, she shrank back again into the waiting-room, intent only on escaping her father's recognition.

Dick Madingley had been also terribly discomposed by the appearance of the banker. He judged it wisest to attract as little attention to himself as possible, and, therefore, instead of lingering, as he had intended, to see Edith emerge from the waiting-room, he got into his carriage and took a seat on the far side from the window. Another two or three minutes and they were off, and Madingley was left to wonder the

whole way up whether his *fiancée* had
effected her escape.

"It could hardly have been a mere
chance," he muttered; "this is some of
Enderby's work, I'll be bound.   I've no
doubt he or his creatures have dogged my
every footstep; he doubtless bribed some
one of my servants to know by what train I
was going to town, and put old Molecombe
up to seeing me off.   His taking his stand
where he did was probably accident, but
there he was like a terrier at a rabbit-hole.
I don't suppose Edith is in the train, she is
a clever and a plucky girl if she managed to
get past him."

On his arrival in London, Mr. Madingley
speedily convinced himself that his surmise
was correct, and, with a furious malediction
on Maurice Enderby, he drove off to the
scene of his usual avocations.

In supposing that the banker's appearance

at the station was due to Maurice Enderby, Dick Madingley was mistaken. It was the result of pure accident. The irascible customer of the day before had called in to have a little more talk with Mr. Molecombe of a less fiery description, and, not having been able to quite finish his say and being at the same time anxious to catch the London train, the banker had walked down to the station with him in order to finish their discussion.

His client off, Mr. Molecombe at once turned his back upon the railway and retraced his steps to the bank. But Edith had no more idea of this than her lover. Conscience-stricken, she thought her premeditated elopement had been discovered, and sat trembling in the most retired corner of the waiting-room, expecting every instant to see her father enter in search of her. When a quarter-of-an-hour had elapsed, and she saw no sign of anyone in quest of her, she ventured to peep once more cautiously out of the door. The platform was nearly deserted; except for a boy cutting papers at the bookstall, and a grimy gentleman assiduously engaged in cleaning lamps, there was no one visible. The very porters were all over on the other side of the line, awaiting the down train.

Edith began to recover her courage. Whatever caused her father's presence there, it was possible, could she only regain her home unnoticed, that her escapade of this morning might be kept a secret. Fortune favoured her, and she regained her own room unnoticed, some quarter-of-an-hour before luncheon, without any one suspecting that she had been beyond the shrubberies.

CHAPTER XIII.

"THE SPOTTED DOG."

TUNNLETON was quite in a ferment during the next day or two. The Torkeslys, the Prauns, and the Maddoxes were much excited about the sudden departure of Richard Madingley.

"Given up his house, by Jove!" said General Maddox in his usual deliberate tones; "paid off all his servants, and has cleared off without beat of drum; hasn't left a P.P.C. card anywhere that I can hear.

Looks queer, sir. Gad, I don't believe that fellow was quite right after all!"

"Right, Maddox!" replied the irascible Praun, who was always in extremes, and who flew from one view to a diametrically opposite one, quickly as the wind flies round the compass, "I have no doubt he was the most confounded impostor that ever put foot in the place. Took us all in, damn his impudence!"

"Very disgraceful, Praun," replied General Maddox, shaking his head; "though, to do him justice, he did give good dinners."

"Yes," replied the other; "and, scoundrel though he was," a remark, by the way, for which General Praun had very scant justification, "I should like to know, before he is hung, where he got his after-dinner sherry; but I don't know what's coming to us: the place is getting turned topsy-turvy; what do you think I passed on my way here? Mrs. Enderby, if you please, driving a carriage and a pair of ponies. Now I hate gossip; I don't want to meddle in my neighbour's affairs, but when you see a phenomenon, such as a curate setting up his carriage and pair, one can't help asking how he does it."

"Livery stable probably," rejoined General Maddox; " trap for the day, you know; two ponies, though? Quite beyond his means," concluded the general, with a shake of his head.

" Means!" cried Praun; " nothing is beyond the means of a gambler while he is in luck. How Jarrow can reconcile it to his conscience, how Tumleton can submit to a parson within its midst, who, instead of attending to his duties, is devoted to speculating on the turf, passes my comprehension!" and in good truth for the next few days the backslidings of Richard

Madingley and Maurice Enderby divided the attention of the town.

But for all that there are not wanting in any community worshippers of the rising sun. To these worldly people that Mrs. Enderby should have turned out a veritable niece of John Madingley and have set up her pony-carriage were signs indicative of coming prosperity that they deemed unwise to neglect. They reminded each other that the Enderbys, although they had said nothing, had always held strictly aloof from Richard Madingley's entertainments: in fact a slight reaction was already setting in in Maurice's favour, although the two generals had by no means abandoned their hostile attitude.

But now that fatal wedding gift once more began to haunt Maurice, once more to send the blood dancing through his veins, once more aroused visions of a broad, green-ribboned turf, white rails, silken jackets, and half a score of horses tearing up "the straight" at full speed. Doncaster meeting commenced in a few days; the sporting papers were, so far, nearly unanimous in predicting that the Wandering Nun would win the Champagne Stakes, and, strive to banish it from his mind though he might, it was all no use, and Maurice Enderby was once more feverishly anxious about the result of the race. He had not dared to ask Grafton to telegraph to him again, although he knew that gentleman would be at Doncaster. The employés at the telegraph office are not altogether reticent about the messages that pass through their hands, and it was pretty well known through Tunnleton that Mr. Enderby had been the first man in the town to know of the Wandering Nun's victory at Goodwood.

Generals Maddox and Praun could hardly

be blamed for holding that Maurice specu-
lated on the turf, for it would be very difficult to have persuaded the Tunnleton people
generally of that, and while the respectable
part of the community regarded a betting
clergyman as an anomaly that could not be
suffered in these days, there was a minor
and godless section who had much admiration
for Mr. Enderby's astuteness. It is hard to
stem the tide of calumny, more especially
when such calumny is based on such apparent grounds as there were in Maurice's
case. His own acts too combined strongly
to strengthen the prevalent belief, the interest he had manifested in racing, the telegram, his sudden command of money, and,
last not least, what his enemies in Tunnleton termed his arrogance and effrontery in
setting up a carriage and pair of ponies.

Most of us have some few sworn friends
who will stand by us unflinchingly should

disaster overtake us, who, if unable to assist
us in our trouble, we know will always meet
us with sincere sympathy and a hearty hand-
grip; there are others who, though loyal
enough in the first instance, begin to waver
as the tide runs high, who begin to calculate
and doubt whether they are prudent in
championing what looks like a lost cause.
Politic and rather timid people some of these
willing to take our part in the first instance,
but afraid that it may be to their own detriment to continue their partizanship when
they find the clouds of popular opinion are
gathering thickly around us. Now this was
rather Mr. Jarrow's case; he had stood
stanchly by Maurice in the first instance,
but even that had not been friendship, but
his natural obstinacy, combined with much
indignation that men like Generals Maddox
and Praun should venture to interfere in
affairs of his. But he was beginning now to

waver in his belief in his curate; evidence
continued apparently to accumulate against
Mr. Enderby, and that Tunnleton gave
credence to such evidence was unmistake-
able. Maurice too declined any explanation,
and, except to the rector, had hardly conde-
scended to deny the accusation brought
against him. Mr. Jarrow began to think
that it behoved Maurice at least to refute the
charge to the utmost extent of his power.
He, the rector, in his interview with Generals
Maddox and Praun had actually blustered
about bringing an action for libel, and yet
Maurice sat down supinely under the scandal,
and made no effort to remove the taint from
his name. The rector was of a pugnacious
disposition, and never happy unless engaged
in a wordy war with somebody, and it was
wormwood to him that Maurice, by the attitude he had taken, precluded all continuance
of his quarrel with the two generals.

In good truth, ever since Grafton had put the idea into his head, which John Madingly had considerably strengthened, Maurice had been weighing in his mind the propriety of his giving up the Church. He had tried it, and, though he had conscientiously performed his duties, still he felt he was in no wise fitted for the profession. He had taken to it as a means of living, but before seeking ordination as priest he felt that a man should have some higher feeling regarding it than that, and now he was once more bitten by the turf fever, and, do what he would, could not keep the "Champagnes" out of his head. The success of the "Wandering Nun" was not the great object which it had been to him when she secured her first victory; he was no longer pressed for money, but nobody exists in such affluent circumstances as not to be very well pleased at the idea of having a little more of that useful

commodity. Still it was not so much that,
as was the interest he took in the career of
the flying filly; and if it had not made a
penny difference to him he would have been
still as deeply interested in the issue of her
forth-coming essay at Doncaster.

The next two or three days slipped by,
and at last came the opening day of the
great Yorkshire meeting, and Maurice knew
that at three o'clock this race, the winner of
which so often made his mark in turf history,
was to be decided. As the afternoon wore
on he could no longer control his restlessness.
They must know it in the town now, the
telegram must have arrived at the club, but
he did not wish to make any further scandal.
He supposed he must wait till he got his
paper the next morning, but he was resolute
not to look in at the club for fear of what
might be said as to his reason for coming
there.

He wandered aimlessly about the town till in an evil moment his vagrant footsteps brought him outside a second-class hotel called " The Spotted Dog." He knew this house by repute, he knew it bore the reputation of being a sporting-house, and he had heard some of the young men at the club declare that they knew what had won a big race at " The Spotted Dog" always a quarter of an hour sooner than anywhere else in Tunnleton. In an evil moment he resolved just to step in and ask the question. He cast a hurried glance up and down the street, but there were not many people moving about, and nobody he knew was in sight. He ran up the three or four steps and glanced rapidly round for some one of whom to make inquiries. A small knot of rather raffish looking young men were gathered in front of the bar, and one of these saved him all further trouble.

"There you are, sir," he said, pointing
to the tissue fastened up in the bar window,
"won in a canter; that 'Wandering Nun'
is about the best bit of stuff Mr. Brooks ever
owned."

Maurice bent his head in acknowledge-
ment of the speaker's civility, and retreated
rapidly into the street, which he gained just
in time to receive a frigid bow from Miss
Torkesly, just issuing from a shop on the
other side of the road. Maurice knew all
was over as he raised his hat. He felt
that Tunnleton would never tolerate this
fresh iniquity, that he would be cast out
from among them. That question of resigning the Church was being much simpli-
fied, as he could not but think, looking back
upon his imprudence. There was much
likelihood of the Church resigning him. It
was well that it was a nice day for walking,
for Miss Torkesly had seldom enjoyed a

busier time than was her lot that afternoon.
To whisper into the ears of all her friends
and acquaintances that she had seen Mr.
Enderby coming out of " The Spotted Dog "
was Miss Torkesly's clear and bounden duty
before she slept.

" So dreadful, my dear. Of course we
all knew that the poor infatuated man gam-
bled, but I'm afraid he drinks as well."

" It is terrible, but I believe they usually
both go together. Fancy, to be seen coming
out of 'The Spotted Dog' in broad day-
light! I didn't know what to do, and I am
afraid I bowed, my dear. Just fancy! bow-
ing to a man who came out of 'The Spotted
Dog.' I was too confused and horrified to
see, but I daresay he was even walking un-
steadily."

Yes, before twenty-four hours were over,
the greater part of Tunnleton was aware of
Maurice's delinquency. About how the unfor-

tunate man left "The Spotted Dog" accounts varied according to the imagination
of the narrator. He was variously described
as being the worse for liquor, having reeled
down the street, or carried home insensible
to his wife. Such a schedule of wrong-
doing as was now filed against Maurice
Enderby was more than a man could hope
utterly to refute.

It was not likely that Mr. Jarrow would
be long left in ignorance of his curate's
questionable proceedings. Mrs. Praun picked
up the news in the course of her afternoon
rambles. The general quite bubbled with
excitement upon hearing of it. "Ah," he
said, "we will see what Jarrow has to say
to this. He took a precious high hand with
me, and threatened me—me! General Praun,
with an action for libel, told me that he had
Mr. Enderby's own word for it that he
never bet upon horses, and, when I pointed

out his sudden plentiful supply of money,
he informed me that he had nothing to do
with that. Mr. Enderby had probably relations who assisted him from time to time.
Ah ! " continued the general, with a trium-
phant snort, " I suppose he was looking for
one of those relatives at ' The Spotted Dog,'
and we shall hear next that his duties neces-
sitate his attendance at a public billiard-room;
but I'll have it out with Jarrow to-morrow
morning."

General Praun was as good as his word.
Habitually an early man, he was at the
rector's house almost as soon as he had
finished his breakfast, and desired to see
him. Shown into Mr. Jarrow's study, he
plunged at once into his subject, and dilated
upon it with such volubility that his as-
tounded host was unable to get a word in.

" I told you so, Jarrow, I have told you
all along, that this paragon of a curate of

yours was a dissolute young man quite unfitted for his position. There is nothing
remarkable in it; you are not the first rector
by many who has been similarly deceived;
but you are so obstinate; you shut your ears
to what your parishioners tell you."

"Obstinate? me?" suddenly interposed the
Rev. Jacob. "If there was ever a man open
to conviction; if ever there was a man pre-
pared to listen to facts or contravention of
his own opinions, I flatter myself I am that
man."

"Very good, then," said General Praun.
"You have been told that Enderby gambles.
You now hear upon unimpeachable testimony
that he frequents what, though he may call it
a second-class hotel, I should denominate a
sporting public. If you think that befitting
one of your cloth well and good, but you
won't find Tumbleton agree with you."

"I need scarcely say," rejoined Mr.

Jarrow, who had by this time somewhat recovered himself, "that I have heard nothing of this before; that I should make inquiry into such a rumour is matter of course."

"It is no matter of rumour, I tell you," snapped Praun, irritably.

"Then, sir," rejoined Mr. Jarrow, in his pompous manner, "it will be so much the easier to investigate. Rumours are difficult to grapple with; facts demand explanation. I shall withhold my opinion till I have spoken to Mr. Enderby on the subject."

And the rather stately bow with which Mr. Jarrow intimated that their interview was at an end made the hot-tempered Praun's very pulses tingle.

"They take too much upon themselves, these parsons. By Jove! Jarrow dismissed me as I used to dismiss a subaltern in the

old days.   Bowed me out as if I had been
a mere nobody instead of a general officer."
And with these thoughts Praun fumed along
on his way to study the daily papers at the
Tunnleton Club.

CHAPTER XIV.

" BETTER I SHOULD RETIRE NOW."

MAURICE told his wife that evening what had happened; and Bessie at first by no means realized the consequence of his imprudence. She did not even know, as was very natural, the name of this second-class hostelry. She did not see that because upon one occasion her husband once entered an hotel it should be looked upon as any great crime on his part. A score of reasons might have taken him there—reasons which might be proclaimed from the house-tops. And it was not until Maurice explained to her that " The Spotted Dog " had the reputation of being a sporting-house, pointed out to her that Doncaster races were going on, and reminded her that he had been charged with betting on horse-racing, and that, though it was not true, his denial thereof had never been half believed in Tunnleton,—that she grasped what would probably be the outcome of this last imprudence.

"Ah, Maurice," she said, " Uncle John meant well, and from a money point of view his gift has proved princely, but I am afraid it will turn out a fatal wedding present in the end."

"You are always saying that," he re-rejoined, testily; " but I think this last escapade is very likely to terminate my engagement at Tunnleton. Jarrow stood by me in the first instance like a thorough gentleman. He took my word that the charge was false, and refused to listen further to what my traducers said, but, looking back, I think that was due in part to the natural combativeness of his nature; moreover, he will very likely tire of perpetually fighting my battles. Do you know, Bessie, I am thinking seriously of giving up the Church."

Now, much as he had thought over this himself, Maurice had never said a word to his wife on the subject, and her first feeling was that of repugnance at the idea. " Oh, Maurice," she said, " you would surely never do that ! "

" Why not ?" he said; "it is surely better that I should retire now than become positively enrolled in a profession for which I feel I am unfitted. I shall never make a good clergyman, but I think I have stuff in me, and could do good work in some other calling."

Still, Bessie was not to be reconciled to the idea; she urged him to consider well what he was about, pointing out that, though he might have been imprudent, he had really done nothing wrong, and that there were other places besides Tunnleton in which he could obtain a curacy.

"Oh, it's a thing that there will be plenty of time to think about. Jarrow is not likely to wish me to leave until he has found some one to supply my place. However, we shall doubtless have some conversation on the subject to-morrow, as a conflagration in a high wind spreadeth not so quick as scandal in the mouth of the Torkeslys."

Maurice had not long to wait. General Praun had left the house not ten minutes when a servant was on his way to Mr. Enderby's with a note, intimating that the

rector wanted to see him as soon as possible. Maurice was quite as anxious for the
interview as Mr. Jarrow, and accordingly
lost no time in making the best of his way
to the rectory. He was admitted at once
to the Reverend Jacob's sanctum, and there
found that gentleman in a most unmistak-
able state of fume and fidget. It was
matter of deep annoyance to Mr. Jarrow
when any *protegé* of his—and he was much
given to taking people up—was found wanting; he prided himself especially upon in-
sight into character, and that his swans
should occasionally turn out geese was
always sore vexation to him. He snatched
greedily at all petty pieces of patronage
which fell at all within his reach; from the
nomination of a pew-opener to recommend-
ing a man as a fit candidate for the town
constabulary, Mr. Jarrow always endeavoured to have a finger in the pie; that any

curate of his should be deemed unfit for his position was casting much discredit on his sagacity.

"Sit down, Mr. Enderby," he remarked, their first greetings over. "I have sent for you upon a very unpleasant business; but the fact has been pointedly brought to my notice, and it is incumbent upon me to ask you for an explanation."

"I will save you all further preamble, Mr. Jarrow," replied Maurice. "You have been told that I was seen coming out of 'The Spotted Dog' yesterday. Perfectly true, I was.—Why did I go in there? To learn the result of a race in which my wife's uncle, John Madingley, had got a horse running. Had I any bets on it? Most certainly not. I never have bet upon horse-racing, except in a very trifling way before I married, and most assuredly I have never wagered a sixpence since on that or anything else."

Mr. Jarrow paused for some minutes before he replied. He thoroughly believed Maurice, but then he felt at the same time that nineteen people out of twenty in Tunnleton would not.

"Mr. Enderby," he said at length, "although I am quite willing to accept your explanation, you must be aware that the public will not. As some eminent man, whose name just now I forget, has said, mistakes are worse than crimes. You must forgive my saying that since you have been among us your life seems to have been a succession of blunders. You have, by your own imprudence, put yourself so completely in the wrong light, that I am afraid it will be impossible to convince the public that you don't gamble, and, from what I heard this morning, they are likely to add drink to your transgressions. I have stood by you as long as I could, but you must excuse my saying," and few would have given the pompous rector credit for the kindliness with which the words fell from his lips, "that, under the circumstances, you can exercise no influence for good in the parish."

"I quite agree with you, Mr. Jarrow," replied Maurice, quickly, "and, as you were doubtless about to say it is better under those circumstances we should part, we will look upon that as clearly understood between us, and I shall remain now only so long as suits your convenience."

"Well, Mr. Enderby, you have taken the words out of my mouth, but I do think that will be the best arrangement we can arrive at. Shall we say, sir, about two months from this date? That will give you time to look round as well as me."

"I have to thank you, Mr. Jarrow," said Maurice rising, " for much kindness since I have been here, and shall be very glad to time my departure with regard to your convenience. As for myself, let me tell you in strict confidence that I have quite made up my mind to resign the profession. And now, for the present, I will say good-morning."

Mr. Jarrow remained for some time after Maurice's departure in a brown study. He shook his head two or three times, like a man who has come across a phenomenon beyond his comprehension. He had had curates resign before now, but this was his first experience of a young man resigning the profession as well as the curacy.

It soon became evident to Maurice that Tunnleton society was unfeignedly shocked at the last scandal in connection with his name. That he should dabble in horse-racing had been deplorable, shocking in the eyes of most people, but a clergyman who

" frequented public houses " (that he had
only been seen entering one once was a fact
quite lost sight of) had put himself quite
without the pale. When Tunnleton heard
that he was going away, it shook its head,
and opined that Mr. Jarrow could do no less.
It was a sad pity that a young man should
be so depraved, but of course he was useless
in his present position, and Tunnleton feared
would do no good any where. And now
curiously enough a reaction set in in favour
of Mrs. Enderby. How it began one hardly
knew, but Bessie had made some few friends
in the place, and it probably owed its origin
to them. It suddenly became the fashion to
express great commiseration for " poor Mrs.
Enderby," and society delighted to paint imaginary pictures of Bessie vainly attempting
to keep her husband in the straight path. It
was difficult to say which suffered most from
the new order of things—Maurice or his wife.

He on his part was subject to the most freezing return to his salutations, but I doubt if that was so hard to bear as the ostentatious pity to which his wife was subjected. Nothing was ever said to her, but the ladies of Tunnleton had determined that she was to be pitied and condoled with, and their faces could not have expressed more mournful sympathy had she been lamenting the actual loss of husband. They both agreed that Tunnleton was unendurable, and Maurice speedily asked Mr. Jarrow to release him as soon as possible.

Two people there were who Maurice determined to take into his confidence. One of these was Frank Chylton, to whom he had already told the story of his singular wedding gift. He now thought it only right to explain to him the itching curiosity that had led him to commit the imprudence of entering "The Spotted Dog." The other was General Shrewster. The latter had

heard the whole story of the wedding present from John Madingley, and the comic
side of the business had tickled him immensely.

"I can understand his reticence," he said,
"but I am afraid it is destined to do him a
good deal of harm here. You see this is an
eminently respectable place, extremely ortho-
dox and all that sort of thing, and when
people are that, they are always not willing
but greedy to believe the very worst of their
neighbours."

But when Maurice told him of this second
imprudence the general simply roared with
laughter.

"My dear Enderby," he said, "how
could you do it ? You know you were, so to
speak, under the ban of Tunnleton, now
you'll be positively outlawed ; what are you
going to do ? You will never make head
against it."

" I am not going to try," replied Maurice
quietly ; " I have resigned my curacy and
am only waiting now as a convenience to
Mr. Jarrow. Further, general, I consider
myself unsuited to the profession, and am
going to adopt some other calling."

" There I think you are right ; it's a
pity that you've thrown away a whole
year, but anything is better than a life-
long mistake. I can only say I shall be
very glad to help you should it at all lie in
my power. As far as ways and means go,
your uncle promised to assist you to a start;
still, I should be afraid his interest would
lie chiefly in the profession you are about
to abandon. For myself, I have none
except in my old trade."

" Thank you very much, general," replied Maurice ; " I will ask for your good
word without fail should I want it, but at

present I have not made up my mind as
to what I shall do."

" Will you let me give you one piece of
advice, the warning of a man who has been
through the furnace: keep clear of the race-
course whatever you do. I was a rich man
once, and should be so now had I not been
bitten by the turf tarantula. I took the
fever very badly, and, unless I very much
mistake, you are a man likely to contract
it in its most virulent form. It makes your
pulses tingle even now, and you will probably be quite carried away if you find
yourself in the thick of the fray. There, I
am going to say no more," said the general,
laughing; " a word is more likely to be
remembered than a sermon in these cases.
Of course my mouth is closed about what
you have told me, but I think the sooner
you allow Chylton and myself to make the
whole story public the better."

"I don't want it published until I am gone," replied Maurice; "I am too angry to care to right myself in the eyes of the people here; and now I will say good-bye for the present."

END OF VOL. II.

www.ingramcontent.com/pod-product-compliance
Lightning Source LLC
Chambersburg PA
CBHW020053030726

47498CB00006B/1760